A DIET TO DIE FOR

Joan Hess

BALLANTINE BOOKS • NEW YORK

Copyright © 1989 by Joan Hess

All rights reserved under International and Pan-American Copyright Conventions. Published in the United States by Ballantine Books, a division of Random House, Inc., New York, and simultaneously in Canada by Random House of Canada Limited, Toronto.

No part of this book may be used or reproduced in any manner whatsoever without written permission except in the case of brief quotations embodied in critical articles or reviews. For information, address St. Martin's Press, 175 Fifth Avenue, New York, N.Y. 10010.

Library of Congress Catalog Card Number: 89-34855

ISBN 0-345-36654-9

This edition published by arrangement with St. Martin's Press, Inc.

Manufactured in the United States of America

First Ballantine Books Edition: April 1992
Fifth Printing: April 1993

FOR BECCA AND JOSH,
WHO PUT UP WITH A LOT OF NONSENSE FROM
THEIR MOTHER.
I LOVE YOU BOTH VERY MUCH.

ONE

The little bell above the door of the Book Depot jangled with such fury I expected to see it sail across the room. It did not. To my regret, two teenage girls sailed across the room and skidded to a halt in front of the counter, where I was thumbing through the checkbook in hopes of something along the lines of what happened on Thirty-fourth Street.

One of them had my curly red hair, green eyes, and pale complexion, and was beginning to be able to look me in the eye without standing on her tiptoes. She was developing some of my mature physical attributes, which led to a great deal of pensive study in the bathroom mirror when she thought I wasn't watching and an artistic display of apathy about the entire business when she realized I was.

The other had limp brown hair, limp brown eyes behind thick lenses, and a limp body that was trapped somewhere between the chubbiness of childhood and a postpubescent promise of sleekness. I suspected her mother had yet to catch her preening in front of a mirror.

"Mother," the former began grimly, "do you want to know what Rhonda Maguire told Inez after fifth period?"

"Not especially," I said truthfully, although I didn't doubt for a second I was going to hear it anyway. My daughter Caron exists on a very intense plane, where nothing simply happens: it explodes, it detonates, it blusters and rages and erupts. Fifteen can do that to you, along with pimples, simmering hormones, and an inability to refrain from eye rolling, lip protruding, and other displays of histrionics. Caron's faithful sidekick, Inez Thornton, has not yet managed to grasp the delicacies of melodrama, but she's a good student and observes Caron's every gesture with wide-eyed awe.

"But it was incredibly gruesome," Inez whispered.

"So's my bank statement," I said.

Caron poked Inez. "Tell her what Rhonda Maguire said. I just want to Absolutely Die every time I so much as think about it. I mean, I thought Rhonda was one of my closest friends, but after what she—"

"What did she say?" I interrupted, bowing to the inevitable.

Inez looked thoroughly miserable, and her voice fell to a raspy whine. "Well, Rhonda said that some of the sophomore football players were watching the fourth-period girls gym class, and . . . and elected Caron . . . Well, they elected her Miss Thunder Thighs of Farberville High School. I didn't think it was the least bit nice. It was, like, really tacky and catty."

I glanced at the newly anointed royalty, who was hyperventilating hard enough to blow a good deal of the dust out the bookstore door. "And we were not amused?"

"No, Mother, we were Not Amused." Out came the lower lip. "I'm glad to know you think it's funny, however." The eyes rolled. "If you'll excuse me, I need to go home and look up suicide techniques in the encyclopedia. Inez, you can have my stuffed animal collection, but only if you swear on your grandmother's urn to tell everyone that Rhonda Maguire has herpes and that she passed it on to the entire football team."

"You look perfectly fine, dear," I said. "Your proportions are quite reasonable for your age."

"That's what you say, but you weren't elected Miss Thunder Thighs, were you?'' she retorted without mercy. ''I'll try not to bloody up the bathroom too badly.''

Inez patted Caron's shoulder. ''I don't see how you can ever show your face at school again. Those football players are all jerks, and Rhonda had no business listening to their crude jokes, much less repeating them to me. She knows I'm your best friend.''

I repressed a sudden urge to leap across the counter and shake two pairs of shoulders. ''I think you're taking this too seriously, but if you're truly upset, then why don't you go on a diet for a week or two and see if that makes you feel better? There's a whole rack of diet books in the self-help section; one of them might be appropriate.''

''It probably won't do any good, but I suppose I could look at them,'' Caron said, iciness now replaced with despondency. She glanced at Inez. ''We can do a diet together. It won't hurt you to lose a few pounds—unless, of course, you prefer to claim the title.''

Inez's mouth pursed as if she were considering a response, but after a moment she nodded meekly and followed Caron around the corner of the rack. I returned my attention to the checkbook, which hadn't produced any major deposits during the minor hiatus, and I was still frowning as the two went past me and out the door, their arms laden with paperback books. I did not suggest anything so crude as payment, but I've always had an aversion to pain.

The afternoon drifted by without any further disruptions, including such annoyances as customers desiring an entire collection of hardbound textbooks. At five-thirty I locked the door of my dusty, musty bookstore and walked up Thurber Street toward my apartment. Caron and I reside in the top half of a house across from the undulating lawn of Farber College. During the winter months we have a fine view of Farber Hall, which in its youth and middle age housed the English department and thus the office of my deceased husband. Carlton had joked about the ceiling coming down on his head, but in the end—his, actually—he should have been more concerned about wet highways and errant chicken trucks.

Passing the sorority house inhabited by nubile young things with a tendency to squeal, I stopped on our front porch to collect my mail. There was no letter from Publishers Clearinghouse mentioning that the check was in the mail. I was glancing through the stack of envelopes with cellophane windows when the downstairs door opened and Joanie Powell joined me.

She was an attractive widow of moderate years, with soft brown eyes and a pleasant smile. On her first day in residence I had learned she lived in Little Rock, worked part time in a travel agency, got along well with her two grown children, and was at the college for a semester to pursue an interest in ceramics. On the second day I had learned she raised azaleas, downed an occasional beer, and had a fondness for barbecued ribs and basketball. I had also learned she was loquacious.

"Why, Claire, I was hoping I'd bump into you," she said as she took her mail from the metal box. Hers, I noticed, was addressed by hand and lacked windows.

"Oh?" I murmured cautiously.

"I wanted to invite you, Caron, and Caron's friend to a little party this weekend. I ran into an old friend of my daughter's, and I thought it would be nice for all of us to get together for tea, cake, and conversation."

"I'd love to, Joanie, but I have to work all day Saturday. My accountant has a tendency toward ulcers, and I feel responsible."

"Then we'll do it Sunday," she said briskly. "Shall we say three o'clock?"

"I don't know about Caron and Inez. They're on one of their typical rampages and may have other plans."

"I do so hope they can join us, Claire. Maribeth is in dire need of companionship, even if for only an hour or so. It took all of my wiles to persuade her to come, and I'd feel bad if no one else could be bothered."

With a brave little sniffle, Joanie went back into her apartment, leaving me to my wretched solitude on the porch. I went upstairs, kicked off my shoes, and, content in the knowledge I'd been manipulated by a master, went into the kitchen for a shot of scotch. I was savoring the serenity of early evening when Caron and Inez thudded into the room, each now carrying a sack from the market.

"We have decided to try the seven-day fruit diet," Caron announced, flourishing a banana. "It's supposed to be absolutely incredible, and you can lose up to ten pounds in one week. Imagine—ten pounds!"

"It doesn't sound healthy," I began in the dreaded maternal tone.

"But it is," Inez inserted. "The first day you eat nothing but bananas in order to enhance your potassium level. Then, on the next day, you eat nothing but oranges, for the vitamin C. On the next day—"

Caron brushed her aside to shoot me one of her finely honed defiant looks. "Actually, it's apples on the second day. They're an excellent source of something or other. Then oranges. I wish you'd pay more attention, Inez; this diet is terribly scientific and we have to do it right if we're going to lose all ten pounds in a week. I for one do not intend to behave like a fruit fly an extra week or two because you got confused about the proper sequence."

"This is scientific?" I said.

"Of course it is," Caron said haughtily. "The guy who made it up is a doctor, for pete's sake. There's a photograph of him on the back cover, and he's wearing a white coat, so he ought to know. Come on, Inez, let's get started."

The two went into the kitchen to put down the sacks, then returned, bananas in hand. I contemplated the wisdom of further discussion centering on nutritional soundness and dubious credentials, but concluded that they were young, healthy, and would survive a week of the crazy diet without any dire side effects. And be safe from scurvy, to boot.

They were nibbling righteously and I was reading the local newspaper when footsteps once again were heard on the stairs. I guiltily began to tell them about Joanie's invitation to the tea party, but then realized the footsteps were masculine and broke off before I reached the essence.

Peter Rosen, a man of great charm and innumerable talents, tapped on the door and came in. He has the curly black hair of a well-groomed poodle, eyes the color of molasses, and a pronounced beak of a nose above fine white teeth. He dresses like a bank president: power tie, three-piece suit, imported footwear, the whole routine. At certain times he and I engage in a mutually enjoyable relationship that veers perilously close to a commitment. At other times, however, it veers perilously close to a precipice—and neither of us are supplied with pitons.

Peter is a cop. He probably would argue that he's a detective in the Criminal Investigation Department of the Farberville police force, but he still has the heart of an old-fashioned, potbellied, nightstick-twirling cop. A cop who feels himself above any assistance from civilians merely doing their patriotic duty to ensure justice for all. A cop who turns splotchy and sputters whenever given a tiny bit of advice from a well-meaning woman with red hair, green eyes, and an acute mind that can solve a mystery and be home in time for the cocktail hour. In the past said woman has been rewarded with acerbity, with acrimony, with accusations that she is a snoop and a meddler.

He gave me an avuncular kiss, then continued into the kitchen and returned with a beer. Once he was settled next to me, he noticed Caron and Inez sharing a chair across the room. "Is the drama club doing a production of *Tarzan*?"

"What's that supposed to mean?" Caron snapped.

"You two look as though you're rehearsing for the role of Cheetah."

"That's so funny I may laugh next week."

"I've never seen you eating bananas," he said mildly. "You're usually eating chips and dip, or pizza, or fries and bacon cheeseburgers. Bananas are healthy."

Caron stuffed the last of hers into her mouth. "Inez and I happen to be on a diet, if you must know."

Peter may have caught a glimpse of my smile, but he assumed the expression of one patently impressed by this manifestation of self-discipline. "That's admirable, but also somewhat of a shame, girls. I spotted a new pizza place out on the highway, and dropped by to invite all of you out for dinner. You two can split the supreme with seven toppings. Claire and I lack the wild abandon of youth, but perhaps we'll risk pepperoni and Italian sausage."

"Make him stop, Mother," Caron said.

"With extra cheese," he continued. "The real gooey kind that you have to rip off with your teeth."

"Mother!"

I patted his arm. "You mustn't tempt them; they're terribly sincere about this fruit regime. Let's leave them to their bananas and try the pizza place ourselves. Furthermore, we can throw octagenarian caution to the wind and order a supreme. If you agree to skip the anchovies, I'll yield on the issue of black olives."

While we negotiated the terms, Caron and Inez whispered intently to each other. Peter and I were on our feet when Caron said, "Inez and I have concluded that it's pointless to begin a diet at night. We're not going to realize the full benefit of the banana day when we've already had all kinds of junk for breakfast and lunch. This diet is meant to be started in the morning."

"So our systems can absorb the potassium," Inez added, her eyes blinking like strobe lights.

"First thing tomorrow morning we'll begin the diet," Caron said firmly.

Inez sounded a shade more dubious as she said, "And have nothing but the allotted six bananas and twelve glasses of water."

"And not one bite of anything else."

On that rationale, we went for pizza.

The following morning I left Caron snoring gently under a comforter and a dozen stuffed animals, and went to do that which makes a minuscule yet nevertheless sincere dent in the national deficit. Saturdays are fairly good for fiction and a smattering of magazines, although the college students remain complacent on weekends and wait until midweek to dash in for study aids. My favorite aged hippie came in for the latest science fiction epic, and we had a grave conversation about the current trend toward fantasy versus old-fashioned carnivorous aliens determined to eat the inhabitants of any or all world capitals. My favorite cop came by with sandwiches. We were discussing various inconsequential things when his beeper beeped. He made a call to headquarters, cast a plaintive look at the remaining half of a turkey on rye, and went away to play detective. In that I am not a snoopy, meddlesome sort, I merely waved and agreed to a movie that night.

I was rearranging the dust in my tiny office and attempting to sneeze my nose off my face once and for all when Joanie called my name from the front of the store. Brushing at my cheeks, I went to see if she was going to allow me to weasel out of her tea party.

She was not. "Good heavens," she murmured, "you look as if you just rode in from a cattle drive. In any case, I wanted to remind you that Maribeth is coming at three o'clock tomorrow, and I'm so thrilled that you and the girls will have the opportunity to meet her. She's a dear, dear girl."

"She's a friend of your daughter's?"

"They met at summer camp when they were twelve, and they were close friends until Maribeth went back east to attend a rather posh, exclusive school. My daughter insisted on a school closer to home." Joanie wandered over to the science fiction rack, but she kept shooting odd little looks over her shoulder at me. "Maribeth has a problem," she said at last.

"So do I," I said promptly. "My bank account. I'm supposed to send in my quarterly self-employment tax by the fifteenth, and I doubt those guys will accept an IOU and half a book of trading stamps."

"Maribeth has a serious problem, Claire, and you're just the one to help her."

"I don't even know her," I said, backing toward the sanctuary of my office, where the danger, in the form of rodents and an allergic reaction to the dust, was more tangible.

"But you will tomorrow. That's why I invited you." She picked up a paperback, then settled it back on the rack and began to stalk me down the aisle. "Maribeth needs to get out, to meet people and do things. She's been back in Farberville for nearly eleven months, and I don't think the poor thing has spoken to a dozen people. She stays home all day every day, just doing housework and watching those silly soap operas on television. What kind of life is that for a twenty-nine-year-old woman?"

I kept moving backward. "Maybe the life she prefers?"

"Nonsense. She's very shy, that's all. Her husband teaches business law at the college, but he's made no effort to include her in the department's social functions. In fact, I suspect he wants her to stay home and iron his shirts. It's important that you and I help her out of her pathetically lonely existence."

We were past the study aids and closing in on the young adult fiction. "If she's married, then it might be a mistake for outsiders to interfere in their relationship," I said, although without much optimism. I'd seen enough of Joanie to know that when she smelled a good cause, she was as stoppable as a freight train coming down a mountainside. "And she really may prefer to stay home. Some people do."

"Oh, Claire, how can you entertain such a silly idea? No, we must encourage Maribeth to take an interest in the outside world. She and I discussed the possibility of her taking a class or two, but she said Gerald—her husband—would never allow it. Even though she would receive a discount on the tuition, she implied they were in a serious financial bind for the rest of this year. Next year will be different, of course, but it may be too late for her by then."

Joanie was baiting me, and we both knew it. Although I am not and never have been snoopy and meddlesome, I do have a healthy curiosity. I stopped in the middle of young adult fiction and said, "You win. What happens next year?"

"She comes into the family money. Didn't I mention that she's the great-granddaughter of Thurber Farber?"

"Thurber Farber?" I echoed, gulping. "As in Farber-ville, Thurber Farber College, Thurber Street, Thurber Farber Memorial Library, and all those other Thurbers and Farbers?"

"Yes, indeed. She's the only direct descendent, although I believe there are a few distant cousins who will receive small amounts from the trust. Maribeth will be a rich young woman on her thirtieth birthday. It's up to us to see that she will also be a happy, fulfilled young woman with a normal life."

I bounced off the young adult fiction and careened into the reference section. "Surely she can borrow against all those millions she'll receive next year?"

"I'm afraid Great-grandfather Farber was a miserly old coot who would have preferred to take it with him, were there an FDIC institution at his final destination. There're several clauses in the trust agreement forbidding early withdrawal, loans, or even using it for collateral. Besides, the lack of money's not the real problem; it's her attitude." Joanie gently untangled me from the metal arm of the rack, brushed a smudge off my nose, and gave me a bright smile. "Well, I'm glad we've got this settled, Claire. I'll be expecting you and the girls at three o'clock."

I was too astounded by the revelation of Maribeth's ances-try to argue, or to wonder how I'd been so helpful when all I'd done was run into a book rack and bruise my fanny. Thurber Farber was quite the local legend. In the thirties, while everyone else was leaping out windows or selling ap-ples on the corner, he'd amassed a fortune dealing in com-modities such as sowbellies and soybean futures. After he had finally made so much money even he was ashamed, he donated enough of it to the tiny town where he'd been born that the town fathers felt obliged to rename most of it after him. He lived the remainder of his life in a grotesquely gothic mansion on the hill overlooking the town, being chauffeured about in a Rolls-Royce and disdaining any contact with the peons.

Thurber Farber's great-granddaughter was going to be

rolling in the green stuff. Wallowing in it like a hog in a mudhole. Using it to wallpaper the dining room and carpet the den. Perhaps, I thought as I picked up the dust rag, she was too intimidated by the idea of all that money coming to her in the future. In any case, I had dust and mouse droppings in my future. Such a glamorous life.

When I dragged home many hours later, I found three banana peels on the kitchen table and a note informing me that Caron and Inez were at Rhonda Maguire's for a bunking party. I put the peels and the note in the trash, took a long bath, and was nearing a civilized mood when Peter arrived.

We greeted each other with a reasonably tempered display of affection, then sat down for a drink before the movie. I told him the maiden name of my soon-to-be-acquaintance, earning a low whistle and a raised eyebrow.

"I hope she becomes your dearest friend," he said.

"She's twenty-nine years old and, apparently, some kind of social misfit who irons shirts and watches soap operas," I said, sighing. "Joanie has decided that she and I are going to save the girl from 'Days of Our Lives' and 'As the World Turns,' not to mention spray starch and permanent-press settings, but she failed to offer further details. It makes me as nervous as a substitute teacher facing a roomful of high-school sophomores."

"Speaking of such beasts, how's the diet going today? Those two ate enough pizza last night to hold them for the duration, and a month or two afterward."

"I haven't seen either of them today. The whole thing's ridiculous. If Rhonda hadn't blurted out the nonsense to Inez, and if Inez hadn't felt some moral imperative to offer an instant replay to her best friend, Caron never would have looked twice at a banana, much less allowed it in her mouth—unless it was adorned with three scoops of ice cream and a quart of hot fudge sauce. I suspect they'll tire of a pizza-free life within a day or two and return to their normal diet of junk food."

I found my jacket and purse, and we opted to walk to the theater, which managed a foreign film every now and then,

along with politically correct amateur theatrics, the annual
local beauty pageant, and other equally desirable produc-
tions. As we strolled down Thurber Street, I idly inquired
about what had occurred earlier that had torn him away from
the turkey on rye.

"A case."

"Anything interesting?" I asked.

"No."

"Goodness, I'm not going to let you teach conversational
skills to Maribeth Farber Whatever. You're positively terse."

"It's official police business," he said in a positively
snooty tone. "If the CID flounders so badly we need your
astoundingly brilliant mind to save us from disgrace, I'll call.
Besides, it really isn't interesting."

"Then I'm not the least bit interested," I said, matching
his tone.

I thought I heard a "Ha!" from somewhere, but I was
hardly in the mood to pursue its origin.

TWO

Caron and Inez staggered in the next morning looking as though they'd had less than an hour of sleep, which was most likely true. A gossipy gaggle of teenage girls is not conducive to a good night's sleep.

I glanced up from the Sunday paper. "Did you have a good time?"

Caron let her sleeping bag fall to the floor. "Yeah, everything was peachy-keen, up until Rhonda felt obliged to tell everybody what those bozos had the nerve to say about me. If that bitch thinks she's ever going to copy my American history notes again, she's got ingrown hairs in her head."

"Nobody laughed," Inez said timidly. "I mean, everybody looked shocked."

"I heard Leslie and Rhonda giggling in the bathroom," Caron continued, glowering at me as if I'd been convulsed over the commode, too.

I opted to change the subject. "So how did the diet go yesterday? Did you eat lots of yummy bananas to elevate your 9potassium?"

Caron folded her arms. "Bananas are gross and disgusting. I never want to look at another banana as long as I live.

13

Inez and I discussed it, and we've decided to try a diet that's not utterly nauseating."

"Yes?" I said encouragingly.

"We're going on the Zen macrobiotic diet. You eat soybeans and seaweed extract and oat bran bread and stuff like that. Ten pounds in ten days. It's terribly healthy."

I repressed a shudder. "You have an interesting definition of the phrase 'utterly nauseating.' Where do you intend to find soybeans and seaweed extract and oat bran?"

"At the health food store. It may be expensive, but we'll only need a ten-day supply."

"The health food store is closed on Sundays," I pointed out. "Since you can't start until tomorrow, you can eat cake with a clear conscience. We're all invited to a party this afternoon."

Inez sadly shook her head. "We really shouldn't. The book says to fast and meditate for a full day before we start the diet. It's supposed to cleanse our systems and align our brain waves for the diet."

"You think I'm going to drink nothing but water and make funny noises through *my* nose all day?" Caron said, curling her lip at the absurdity of such a suggestion. "I happen to have a very delicate metabolism. If my blood sugar drops below a certain level, I get totally dizzy. I have no intention of being dizzy all day today when I have to study for an algebra test second period tomorrow." Having dealt with that, she turned on me. "Whose party and what kind of cake?"

"Mrs. Powell in the downstairs apartment, and I don't know what kind of cake. She looks like the sort who'll serve several kinds, though, and all made from scratch."

Caron nodded, then poked Inez into motion. "Come on, let's make waffles. Those petrified doughnuts Rhonda produced this morning were at least a week old. I seriously considered suggesting to Rhonda that we use them to play a variation of horseshoes—using her sweet little button nose for a stake."

The two devoted dieters left me in peace.

By three o'clock I'd read every word of the newspaper except for the sports section and the classifieds, being less than fascinated by neckless hulks and hot deals on used cars. I had not come across anything that might relate to Peter's newest case, but I decided it would be in the following day's edition. The girls came out of Caron's room and we dutifully trooped downstairs.

Joanie seemed edgy as she invited us in. "Maribeth's not here yet," she said to me in a low voice. "I'm worried that she panicked and decided not to come, or that her husband refused to allow it. Do you think I should telephone her?"

"She's only a minute or two late, Joanie. It's too early to call the CID and report her missing."

"You're right, but I'm still concerned. She's terribly shy. However, all we can do is hope she arrives shortly. In the interim, let's all have some tea and cake."

Caron and Inez were already admiring the silver tea service and the platters of goodies on the coffee table. Joanie served us, then poured herself a cup and sat down, managing to check her watch every thirty seconds without spilling a drop or a crumb. Caron and Inez made a mockery of the proposed fast by taking several slices of all three cakes, along with discreet handfuls of cookies and a sprinkling of salted nuts.

I admitted to myself that I was curious about the mysterious Maribeth Whatever née Farber. I was in the midst of imagining a wide-eyed fawn poised on the front porch, her hand flirting with the doorbell, when the doorbell jangled.

Joanie hurried to the door and opened it. "Why, Maribeth, I'm delighted that you could come this afternoon. I invited a few friends to join us, and they're looking forward to meeting you. Now come right in; I insist."

The fawn had wide eyes. She also had a body with an excess of at least a hundred pounds. I tried not to stare as Joanie took Maribeth's wrist and pulled her across the room to introduce us, saying, "Maribeth, this my upstairs neighbor, Claire Malloy, who owns that wonderful bookstore in the old train depot. Claire, this is Maribeth Galleston."

"I'm pleased to meet you, Maribeth," I managed to say in what I prayed was a normal voice. She had a heart-shaped face that would have been quite pretty had it not been as misshapen and pasty as leavened bread dough. Her dull brown hair was pulled back in an uncompromisingly tight ponytail. Her eyes were the palest blue I'd ever seen, and ringed with thick curly lashes. Her faded, shapeless dress had seen too many seasons, or perhaps too many sessions in the washing machine, and it was very snug, accentuating her bulging stomach and broad rear end.

She gave me a weak smile, and, after a gulp that sounded painful, said, "It's nice to meet you."

Joanie kept her hand around Maribeth's wrist as she shot Caron and Inez a level look and said, "This is Claire's daughter Caron and this is Inez Thornton. You girls are in tenth grade, right?"

Caron took in a deep breath as if preparing to make funny noises through her nose. To my relief, she let it out silently and said, "Pleased to meet you, Maribeth. Yeah, we're in tenth grade. Farberville High School." Beside her, Inez made a weak sound meant to second the sentiment.

Maribeth looked a little brighter. "I went to school in Farberville, but then I went away to college on the East Coast. I always wondered if I might have enjoyed the local college more."

Joanie suggested she sit down next to me. After more tea had been poured and the platters passed, she said, "I'm so glad you came, Maribeth. When you were late, I was worried that your husband might have had other plans for the afternoon."

Maribeth's teacup rattled in her saucer, and her laugh was unconvincing. "Oh, Gerald had plans for the afternoon. He's playing racquetball with one of his friends from the department. I used to go along to watch, but the sight of all those svelte bodies got to me after a time or two. Besides, there's usually an old movie on the television on Sunday afternoons. I'd rather stay home than be the object of whispers and giggles."

The silence was such we could have heard a cockroach sneeze. Caron and Inez began to stuff cookies in their mouths, while I discovered the necessity of stirring my tea. At last, when the bottom of my porcelain cup was in danger of being scratched for all eternity, Joanie cleared her throat and said, ''And what did you take your degree in, Maribeth? Did you continue your interest in art history?''

''I had to drop out my senior year.''

''How unfortunate,'' Joanie murmured. ''Perhaps you could finish your degree here at Farber College. The art department has a degree program in art history, and you might even look into the possibility of a graduate degree.''

Maribeth gazed at the wall above Joanie's head. ''There's not much point in finishing my degree. Gerald expects to be offered tenure when he publishes his book on international business law, and he'll want me to stay home in order to manage the house and entertain. He thinks it's important for professors to maintain a certain life-style, because of the competitiveness within the department. Besides, there's not much I can do with a degree in art history. Outside of teaching, the only option is a job in a museum or a gallery, and Farberville has neither of those.''

We once again found ourselves straining to hear a wee nasal eruption from the kitchen cabinets. This time Caron rescued us. ''This cake is swell, Mrs. Powell. It's kind of our last chance to eat anything sweet for ten days, because Inez and I are going on a diet first thing in the morning. It's this wonderful macrobiotic thing where . . . you . . .'' Her voice dribbled into nothingness as she realized what she'd said, and her face flushed until it might have been mistaken for a cherry tomato. ''I didn't mean that—that—well, I didn't mean anything. I'm sorry if anyone thought I meant anything.''

''She never means anything,'' Inez contributed helpfully.

Maribeth continued to gaze serenely at the wall, but her cup again began to rattle against her saucer, and her eyes seemed overly bright.

Joanie said, ''I was reading about a new diet place in town, called the Ultima Center. It's on the other side of the campus in that open mall just off the bypass, and they claim to have a foolproof plan with a money-back guarantee. Those programs can be expensive, but they do work for some people, so they may be worth it.''

"Really?" Maribeth said with only a flicker of inflection.

I glanced at my watch. "My goodness. It's getting late, and I promised myself I'd go down to the store and spend several hours unpacking the latest shipments. There's no way I can get to them during the week, and Sundays are my only opportunity to work without constant interruptions. Caron, you and Inez can come help me for an hour or two. It'll help cleanse your systems and align your brain waves for the upcoming ordeal.''

"What you need is a part-time clerk," Joanie inserted before the girls could rally an argument. "Think how much you could get done if you had someone to mind the front of the store, if only for a few hours every afternoon. Without all those interruptions you'd be able to stay in the office and balance the books or unpack shipments, that sort of thing.''

I realized why the fox had insisted on serving tea in the henhouse. "It would be extremely helpful, Joanie, but the unpleasant truth is that I can't afford to hire someone for thirty minutes, much less on a regular part-time basis. If you don't believe me, I'll bring you a note from my accountant—and I can assure you it'll be written in red ink. But thanks for the suggestion; I'll keep it in mind in the event that the general populace takes up literacy as a hobby some day in the distant future.''

"Part-time help shouldn't be all that expensive," she continued, as determined as a compulsive gambler on a roll. "Even as little as two hours a day would allow you to get all sorts of things accomplished. I'm sure it would be worth the minor expense.''

"Maybe at a later time," I said with all the vagueness I could produce. "For the moment, I'll have to settle for indentured labor from my darling daughter and Inez, who need to earn enough money to keep themselves in seaweed extract for ten days. Thanks for the tea and cakes; they were quite delicious. Nice to have met you, Maribeth. Perhaps the Guggenheim will open a branch one of these days.''

Motivated by my beady stare, Caron and Inez mumbled thank-yous and nice-to-have-met-yous, and we fled to the Book Depot before Joanie could propose the name of the perfect candidate to rescue me from myself, even if I preferred otherwise.

When we'd done all we could bear to do, I told the girls I would treat them to a final meal and we went up the hill to a charmingly inexpensive Mexican restaurant that served killer fajitas. Caron perused the menu with a morose frown, then looked at Inez, who had a similar (although somewhat tepid) expression. ''You know, we're not going to be able to start this macro thing tomorrow morning, because we can't stock up until after school. We'll have to wait until Tuesday morning, which means I'll be Miss Thunder Thighs an extra day.''

I sensed a pattern in the making, but being both weary from physical labor and leery of the possibility of being coerced into paying a part-time employee with that which I normally used to pay the rent, I opted not to say as much and took refuge in a frozen margarita. The girls ordered cheese dip and extra chips.

The following morning Caron, fully caught up in the role of a convict on death row, ingested several thousand calories for breakfast and dragged herself off to school, muttering all the while about impending humiliation and the possibility of dropping out to become a clerk at a discount clothing store. It was almost moving. I tidied up and dragged myself off to the Book Depot, muttering all the while about impending bankruptcy. It was incredibly moving.

The day was less than frantic, and I was rearranging the romance novels when Joanie came into the store, put her fists on her hips, and said, ''Well? Have you spoken to Maribeth yet?''

''I can't afford to hire her.''

''Nonsense, Claire. It's obvious that the poor girl will do

nothing if we don't give her some help. I thought I could rely on you, and I must say I'm disappointed.''

"If you won't read my lips, at least read my bank statement. I don't have anything remotely resembling minimum wage with which to hire a part-time clerk. I'd like to help Maribeth, but I simply can't do anything until business picks up. I usually have a rush before Christmas; I'll certainly keep her in mind if I find that I can hire someone.''

"She may be beyond help by then," Joanie said, clearly unwilling to read anything. "After you scurried away yesterday—and in a very cowardly manner, I might add—Maribeth and I discussed the possibility of her trying the Ultima Center. She agreed that it sounded promising, but insisted that she couldn't afford it and that her husband would be furious if she borrowed the money from me or anyone else. The solution is as clear as the front window of this store." She winced at the patina of dust on said window. "Clearer," she corrected herself. "Maribeth must earn the money herself. Here, working part time for you.''

Had my red hair not been so alluring, I might have ripped out great swatches of it in frustration. "I cannot afford her. Maybe in December. Hell, maybe in November, if the professors decide to throw extra reading material at the freshman lit classes. But until that happens, or the borders of hell start icing over—no way. I'm sorry, but that's all there is to say about it.''

"Then I'll pay her salary. We'll just keep that our little secret. You give Maribeth a call and ask her if she can start immediately. That way she can also begin the Ultima program and shake off this dreadful lethargy.''

"I can't let you do that.''

Joanie came across the room and stuck her face about three inches from mine. "Either allow me to pay her salary or pay it yourself. This girl was a dear, dear friend of my daughter's, and I am determined to do whatever is necessary to restore her body and her spirit. When the girls were in junior high, Maribeth used to visit us over all the holidays and a good part of the summer. She was a tiny bit plump, but she had a quick wit and a laugh that reminded me of sunlight reflected on a pool of water. She was filled with energy, and she was always coming up with crazy schemes that kept them in mild trouble and me in semihysterics. Now she's dull and depressed, unable to leave the house or take an interest in anything beyond brownies and daily doses of serialized melodrama.''

I thought of a few debatable points, none of which would have done the slightest bit of good, and ceded with a shrug. ''Okay, you can pay her salary for a month or so. I've got more than enough for her to do—if she's willing. Have you discussed this potential employment with her?''

''Of course not. She would be deeply suspicious if I said one word about it. You must call her, or better yet, run by her house and plead with her. Tell her how desperate you are for help, and how perfect she is to handle the counter while you fiddle around in the back. And you must sound convincing, Claire—she's quite bright and more than capable of spotting any lack of enthusiasm on your part.''

The lecture continued in this rut until Joanie had satisfied herself I could follow her rigorous instructions. I cravenly agreed to drive by the old Farber house after I'd closed for the day but was informed that the issue demanded immediate action. After another round of futility, I left Joanie behind the counter and drove across town and up the hill to Farber Manor, now the Galleston residence.

I'd always been intrigued by the house, which from its vantage point seemed to loom over the local goings-on with an uncompromisingly grim sneer. It was three stories high and painted in an unappealing shade of mustard, with swooping gables, peeling gingerbread trim designed by a leaden hand, and lanky windows that were shuttered to turn away any curious glances from the street. The wrought-iron gates were closed but not locked, and once I'd shoved them aside and mopped the sweat off my face, I drove up the weedy driveway and parked in front of the broad porch. There were no other cars in sight. Wondering if Maribeth were home (or had deduced Joanie's plot and disappeared), I rang the door-bell.

The noise echoed as if in a bottomless well, as if the sound waves were careening off unadorned walls and swirl-ing through cavernous, empty rooms long devoid of life. After a moment, I concluded no one was home and started back to my battered little hatchback. As I reached the bottom step, the door opened behind me.

"Claire?"

"Maribeth," I said, turning back without, I dearly hoped, visible reluctance. "I wasn't sure you were here, since I didn't see any cars."

"I don't go anywhere, so there's not much point in having a second car."

Her voice was as flat as it had been the previous afternoon when Joanie was extolling the virtues of the Ultima Center, but her fingers gripped the side of the door with white inten-sity and her pale blue eyes were glittering with some unfath-omable emotion. I would have given anything I possessed, except my keen mind and brilliant deductive powers, to climb into my car and drive away, but I knew that if I did, I'd also have to face Joanie Powell. I ordered myself to smile. "May I come in for a moment? I have a proposition for you."

"Gerald will be home for lunch any minute. He usually brings papers to grade or a book to read, and he doesn't like to be disturbed."

"I promise not to lie on the dining room table," I said, intending to insert a note of levity but realizing I'd managed to sound like an escapee from a state institution. "I'll discuss this with you as quickly as possible and try to be gone by the time your husband arrives."

"I suppose it's all right," she said, then stepped back and gestured for me to enter the oppressively dark foyer that brought to mind the House of Usher.

I followed her down a corridor to an enormous kitchen. It was somewhat lighter, but still shadowy and unnerving, as were the massive black fixtures and faded brown wallpaper.

She sat down at a dinette and said, "Can I get you coffee or anything?"

"No, I'm in a hurry myself. After listening to Joanie's remarks about hiring a part-time person, I decided she was right. Every time I sit down to do the accounts or sort through invoices, a customer wanders in and forces me to put down whatever I'm doing. By the time I get back to it, it's as if I'd never seen it before. I wondered if I might persuade you to come in for a couple of hours each afternoon and basically hold down the front of the store for me."

She clasped her hands together and gave me a look that hinted of fear. "I couldn't. It's out of the question."

"It's not a difficult job, Maribeth. You'll have to familiarize yourself with the basic layout so that you can help customers on occasion, but most of them are regulars who know what they want and where to find it. My cash register's only a few years older than the American Revolution and easy to operate. Ring up the sale, put the book and receipt in a bag, and that's all there is to it."

"I couldn't." She looked as if she were going to continue, but flinched as a door slammed in the distance. With another frightened look in that direction, she struggled to her feet and went across the room to an oversized refrigerator of my cash register's era.

"Is that Gerald?" I asked brightly, if not brilliantly.

"I haven't even started his lunch. He's only got an hour, and he's upset if everything's not on the table the minute he walks into the kitchen. But I'm out of almost everything, and he hasn't done any grocery shopping for more than a week." Her voice was becoming increasingly shrill as she began to grab containers from the interior shelves. "He doesn't like leftovers; I eat them myself and prepare something fresh for him. Oh, *damn*. I've got a slice of ham in here somewhere."

The kitchen door opened and a black-haired man came into the kitchen. He wore a conservative suit and a dark tie, and his shoes shined as if they'd been coated with enamel-based paint. His body was the antithesis of Maribeth's; it was obvious he was the Jack Sprat who scorned fat. Everything about him was thin, including his lips and hooded eyes. Because of his pronounced cheekbones and concave cheeks that converged on a rather weak chin, his face had an element of felinity about it that I found unappealing. I suspected I was in the minority.

"Gerald," Maribeth said in a startled voice. "I'll—I'll have your lunch in a minute. This is Claire Malloy. She owns a bookstore near the campus, and she—ah, she came by for a brief visit. I'll show her out and fix something for you."

He crossed the room to examine me. After a moment, he produced a smile and said in a voice that would have worked well in a Pennzoil commercial, "How nice of you to visit Maribeth. Please don't leave on my account; it's rare that anyone can endure her company."

Maribeth's shoulders twitched, but she kept her back turned. Mimicking his oily voice, I said, "I appreciate your concern for my well-being, but I enjoy Maribeth's company."

"There's always a first," he murmured, managing to imply he felt sure I was a likely candidate for a lobotomy. "Well, I certainly don't want to interrupt this cozy little chat, so I'll pick up a sandwich on my way back to school. Maribeth, do you need anything from the market? In that I'm forced to eat junk food for lunch, I would appreciate a decent meal this evening."

"I made a list yesterday. It's in my purse in the front room." He crossed his arms and stared at her until she began to fidget.

"I'll go get it," she mumbled and trudged out the kitchen door.

Gerald snorted. "She's hardly a beacon in the night. You, to the contrary, seem to have a functional mind inside your admirably sleek and attractive body. Which bookstore is yours?"

"The Book Depot on Thurber Street. It's a handful, but I enjoy it most of the time," I said, determined to be civil while secretly envisioning him floating face down in a sewage ditch. ''Maribeth mentioned yesterday that you're writing a textbook.''

''It's nearing completion, and I'm quite pleased with it. I hope I don't sound too much like a proud father, but I feel it will be the definitive text on the development of international trade regulations in the late nineteenth century.''

''It sounds fascinating,'' I lied. ''And you teach international law at the college, Maribeth said. Where did you take your law degree?''

''Back East,'' he said vaguely. ''What in God's name is taking Maribeth so long? I've got a class in less than forty-five minutes, and I'm already off schedule because she couldn't bother to fix my lunch. Now it seems she can't find her purse.'' He frowned at his watch, which I noticed was of double-digit carats. ''Listen, Claire, be a doll and tell Maribeth I've gone back to school. She can waste the rest of the day searching for the list, should she run out of more important things to do. Perhaps one of these days you and I can get together and discuss the publishing business over a drink. I'm sure it would be an intriguing conversation.''

He gave me a smile that implied we'd discuss other things, too, and went out of the kitchen. I heard his voice in the hall, with pauses during which Maribeth must have spoken, followed by the slamming of the door and seconds later the sound of a car engine.

The man was a bully and as much of a jerk as any opinionated member of the sophomore football team. However, when Maribeth came into the room and sat down across from me, I merely said I hoped my presence hadn't caused too many problems.

''He's always like that,'' she said dully. ''He gets so impatient with me that I end up flustered and helpless. He's right when he says I'm incapable of doing anything except adding pounds every week. I suppose one day I'll explode and he can find some skinny little coed with a major in nuclear physics, a minor in microbiology, and a shelf full of racquetball trophies.''

She was attempting to sound flip, but her face crumpled

like a punctured soufflé and she began to cry. I patted her hand and made ineffectual noises until she stopped crying and blew her nose resoundingly. I then said, "That's why you need to take a part-time job at the Book Depot, Maribeth. I'm confident you'll make enough money to enroll at this Ultima diet place and start doing something about your weight problem. If you don't do something, you're going to have some serious medical complications, not to mention emotional ones. Joanie said you were bright. Why don't you act like it, for pete's sake!"

"Gerald won't allow me to work. He says it's inappropriate for a professor's wife to have a job, because everyone would assume his salary is inadequate to support us. It's vital that publicly we look as if we're in the same financial bracket as his colleagues, even if it means scrimping along in private. Maybe I'll try this diet place next year, when I come into some money."

"I could talk to Gerald. He's surely concerned about your health, and I don't think helping out at a bookstore is equivalent to mopping someone's floors or clerking in a convenience store."

She rubbed her forehead, sighed, and said, "He'll never allow me to have a job, even if it's respectable. Thanks for the offer, Claire . . . and tell Joanie thanks for me."

"Joanie has nothing to do with this. I need help at the store and you need the money. You've had jobs before, haven't you?"

She gave me a blank look. "No."

"Didn't you baby-sit or something?"

Her cheeks turned pink and she found something of interest to gaze at in her lap. "My family was well off. If I wanted pocket money, all I had to do was ask. The money's tied up now, but I'll assume control of the bulk of it next year on my birthday."

"That's nothing to be ashamed of, Maribeth. On the other hand, it's no excuse to sit in this dreary house all day because your husband doesn't want you to get out and do things. You're not a scullery maid. You're young and intelligent and capable of taking charge of your life.'' I was frothing by this point, but for a good cause.

I'd taken a deep breath and prepared myself for round two (or three—I'd lost count), when she said, ''It would be nice to see someone once in a while. I was going to join the Law Wives Auxiliary, but Gerald wouldn't let me. He said it would embarrass him.''

If I'd possessed a lethal weapon and a propensity for violence, I would have driven straight to the law school and gunned Gerald down in front of the class, thus provoking a lively and informative discussion about justifiable homicide. Instead, I said, ''If you're willing to work every afternoon from two until four, it would be a tremendous help to me. At least promise me that you'll think about it, okay?''

''I'll think about it,'' she said morosely and without any discernible conviction.

I told her to call me later. She walked me to the front door and was still standing in the doorway as I got in my car and drove down the driveway. She looked as despondent as I felt.

THREE

I drove back to the store and repeated the conversation I'd had with Maribeth, mentioning that I'd also met Gerald. Joanie was not impressed with my efforts. After a few minutes of communicating as much, she announced she had not yet abandoned all hope and that she was going to the Ultima Center to pick up information about the program and its cost. I warned her not to sign anything she couldn't read without a magnifying glass and, with a small sigh of relief, watched her drive away.

As predictably as the 1040 forms arrive the week after Christmas (ho, ho, ho), Caron and Inez stormed the store at four o'clock.

"We have been to that health food store," the former announced. The latter blinked in support.

I closed the checkbook and aligned my pencil (red) beside it. "Were they running a special on kelp?"

"I have no idea what you're talking about, Mother," Caron said in a tone meant to convey there were More Important Things on the agenda than obtuse remarks from her mother. "Do you know how much they want for one little packet of yellowish-green stringy stuff that looks like dried dog hair?''

"Your firstborn child?''

"This is not funny.'' Caron glowered at Inez; Inez nodded her head, realized that might not be the requisite response, shook her head, and finally gave up and stared at the floor. "They want an absolute fortune. I pointed out that it was just icky seaweed and that no one in his or her right mind would eat it unless going on a macrobiotic diet, and the guy got all snooty and said he ate it every morning for breakfast. On rice cakes. And drank goat's milk.'' She stopped to roll her eyes as she relived the repugnant scene. "Well, I told him that his store was a total rip-off and that he ought to be arrested for public indecency for having pornographic food right there on the counter where innocent children might see it.''

I held up my hand. "And he threw you out of the store, and therefore you have no way to go on the macrobiotic diet. How am I doing?''

It was obvious I wasn't in contention for any popularity awards, or even a nomination. Caron mentally ran through her repertory and settled on the role of martyred teen-saint. "I was only trying to improve myself,'' she said as her eyes filled with tears. "Today Rhonda told Inez that Louis Wilderberry, who's so stupid he wears his IQ on his football jersey, said the guys were making me a cardboard crown and one of those stupid sashes. I could just die.''

"It's terrible,'' Inez added in a sepulchral voice.

Caron covered her face with her hands, either out of despair or a desire to win an Oscar. "When I grow up—if I decide to—I'll probably end up like that Maribeth person. I'll have to wear clothes made out of polyester bed sheets and no one will let me sit on wicker furniture. I might as well call it quits while I can still fit into a prefab coffin.

At this point whatever patience I had evaporated. "Now listen here,'' I said angrily, "Maribeth has a legitimate problem, and she doesn't whine nearly as much as you do. If you don't want to be grounded for the next five years while you ponder the value of compassion, cut out that kind of thoughtless remark and stop this self-indulgent moaning and groaning. Give up pizza and sodas and chips and cupcakes for two weeks and you'll lose a few pounds. Take the money you were going to use for seaweed and send anonymous boxes of Twinkies to Rhonda Maguire so she can be Miss Fabulous Flab or whatever.''

"Miss Thunder Thighs," Inez corrected me politely.

Caron's eyes narrowed to slits and her lower lip popped out like the plastic doneness indicator in a roasted turkey. "Come on, Inez, there are half a dozen more diet books at my house. We didn't even look at the one where you mix up things in a blender."

I waited until the poor little bell jangled, then leaned back in my chair and tried to determine when and where I'd gone wrong, or how I could have gone so very wrong. Dr. Spock had smiled at me from the bedside table. I'd read those magazines in the pediatrician's office, the ones crammed full of articles on how to teach baby to be bilingual and how to recognize common illnesses before any symptoms appeared. I'd taken pictures at all her birthday parties and had sworn to have the roll developed before she went away to college. Then again, I hadn't checked her into a nunnery on her thirteenth birthday.

I was wondering if there might be a nunnery in the immediate area when the bell jangled me out of my reverie. I went to the front room and found Peter Rosen thumbing through a magazine.

"How's the diet going?" he asked.

"They talk a good line, but thus far they've managed to avoid actually going on any of them. I finally got fed up with their incessant excuses and suggested they cut out junk food for two weeks. I might as well have suggested they sprout halos and audition with the pope for beatification."

"Every once in a while I wonder if I should have begat a child to take care of me in my old age. Then I take a hard look at your offspring and put a few dollars in my savings account. When I'm in my dotage, you'll feed me oatmeal and wipe the drool off my chin, won't you?''

"If they give us adjoining rooms at Sunset Manor," I said lightly. It was time for a diversion. "I didn't see anything in the newspaper about this new case of yours."

"And you never will."

"Then you're not involved in anything?"

"Oh, but I am, and it's a major muddle. All I said was that you'd never read about it in the paper."

"So it's terribly hush-hush? Classified information, the CIA, Farbergate; that sort of thing?"

He gave me a wolfish grin. "Your nostrils are flaring, darling. Could it be you're curious?"

"Of course not," I said, mentally cursing my tattletale nostrils. "I merely wanted to know if you were going to be occupied with this case for the next few days."

"Why would I assume otherwise?" he murmured.

"Why don't you go away and assume whatever you want. I have better things to do than indulge in this silly conversation. You're not at all attractive when you gloat."

He gave me a wounded look. "I wasn't gloating. This happens to be one case you'll never read about, that's all. For once you won't be able to interfere, and I take a vast pleasure in that."

I was considering how much acidity to insert into my next comment when the telephone rang. I settled for a tight-lipped smile, picked up the receiver, and said, "Book Depot."

"Claire?"

It was almost a whisper, and I had no problem identifying its origin. "Maribeth, what a pleasant surprise."

"I've been thinking about what you said, and if you're still willing to hire me, I guess I'd like to work part time."

"That's an even more pleasant surprise. Are you sure it's not going to cause problems with Gerald?"

"It'll cause problems with Gerald," she said in a resigned voice, "but I don't know that I care. Not caring's become a habit lately. When shall I start?"

"Tomorrow would be fine. Since you have no transportation, I'm sure Joanie will be happy to pick you up and bring you to the store. She adores to volunteer.'' I said good-bye and hung up. Feeling more than a little bemused, I repeated my suggestion to Peter that he make assumptions elsewhere.

He wandered away, still grinning like a damn wolf giving directions to a red-hooded kid, and I was trying to figure out how to find out about his mysterious case when Joanie returned.

''Were you impressed with the diet place?'' I asked.

''Very much so.'' She nudged me off my stool and sat on it. ''It's only been open a few weeks, and they're offering a special to get started. It's owned and run by a young doctor named Sheldon Winder and his wife, Candice, who's a registered nurse. They both seem very professional. Dr. Winder does a complete medical history and examination, then orders whatever tests he feels are necessary to make sure the client won't have any ill effects from the program, which is quite strict and rigorous. Then Candice or another staff member meets daily with the client to monitor urine samples and blood pressure.''

''How much does this attention cost?''

Joanie tried to look nonchalant. ''That's determined by the length of the program and the desired weight-loss goal.''

''In Maribeth's case?'' I said, unimpressed.

''With the initial examination, the required EKG and blood work, the daily vitamins and potassium supplements, the protein packets, and the weekly behavior modification classes?''

''With all of the above. How much?''

''Oh, Candice estimated somewhere in the range of six to seven hundred dollars, but the program is guaranteed as long as the client doesn't cheat.''

I had to grab the edge of the counter to steady myself. ''Seven hundred dollars? You've got to be kidding.''

''And fifteen a week for the exercise classes at the fitness center next door,'' she added with a wince. ''I was a little appalled, myself, but I'm committed to helping Maribeth, and I'll write you a check so that you can advance the money to her. Her appointment is tomorrow at four-thirty.''

''Why are you so positive she'll agree to any of this? I told you that she wasn't exactly overcome with delight at the idea.''

''Because I called to tell her I'd signed her up and that the only way she could pay Ultima was to take the part-time job here. I may have mentioned something about collection agencies and small claims court if she failed to honor the contract.''

''Nothing you signed is binding on her. Maribeth may have panicked, but Gerald's a lawyer and he's not going to fall for an idiotic play like that.''

''I don't think,'' she said pensively, ''that she fell for it, either. I think she pretended to in order to allow someone to make the decision for her, to remove the responsibility from her and perhaps divert some of Gerald's displeasure. In any case, once I take her there tomorrow, she'll sign a new contract and have no choice.''

''I hope you don't ever decide to take me under your wing. You're not a mother hen—you're a turkey vulture.''

''How inordinately kind of you,'' she said, then slid off the stool and left, her expression resembling that of a particular vulpine cop.

When I arrived home I found Caron and Inez huddled over the blender. The table was littered with an amazing number of ingredients, including a milk carton, eggshells, several small bottles, and the cocoa tin. I left them to watch their potion spin and was lounging in the bath when Caron called through the door that they were going to a pep rally at school.

Caron made it back at a reasonable hour, announced she was totally swamped with mindless geography homework because Coach Dooley was a tyrant without enough brains to prepare lesson plans and therefore assigned pages and pages of dumb things just so the students could correct them in class. I made sympathetic noises and was rewarded with a peaceful evening while she hid out in her bedroom. Grousing on the telephone with Inez, naturally.

The following afternoon, Joanie delivered Maribeth to the store and reminded her of the four-thirty appointment at Ultima. I gave Maribeth a quick tour, showing her how the cash register worked and where to record orders if a book was not in stock. Neither of us mentioned Gerald, and I left her standing behind the counter, her face bleak for someone making at least five times as much an hour as I did.

Joanie returned at four and whisked Maribeth away to commit to a seven-hundred-dollar contract and the cheery prospect of months of inedible greenery, potassium supplements, and daily urine samples. Minutes later Caron and Inez came by, announced that they had finally found the absolute perfect diet, hung about until I agreed to give Caron an advance of her allowance (which happens so often I don't owe a dime until the next century), and allowed themselves to be shooed out the door.

When the local paper was delivered by a pimply boy who evinced animation only on collection days, I pored through the main section in hopes of finding some insignificant article that hinted of criminal activity significant enough to warrant the attentions of the CID. To my chagrin, Farberville seemed to be gripped by a wave of lawfulness, except for the usual stuff. Cars were being deprived of their radios and tape decks. Mailboxes were being spray-painted and/or bashed. Students were being admitted to the emergency room after resolving disputes with rednecked troglodytes behind the bars on Thurber Street. Purses left on tables in nightclubs were being harvested by unknown hands.

But I could find no mention of any serious crimes. Petty theft, student bashing, and vandalism were hardly earth-shattering; a sudden drop in the numbers might have been greater cause for alarm.

Peter's smug demeanor was more than a little irritating. He'd described the case as a major muddle, which implied some sort of felony, or at least the possibility of one. Although I had no intention of interfering with his officious official investigation, I damn well wanted to find out what was going on, if only to prove I could. I allowed myself to imagine the scene in which I casually mentioned the gist of the case, then told him I found it less than worthy of my time and energy. The scene was so savory I could almost taste it.

A delightfully devious ploy came to mind. I dialed the telephone number of the CID, identified myself, and sweetly asked to speak to Peter. The gods were rooting for me, for I was informed that Lieutenant Rosen was out of the office. Grinning in anticipation, I asked where he could be reached.

"Well, I'm not supposed to give out that information," the desk sergeant began in a drawl, "but since it's you, Mizz Malloy, I don't see how it'd hurt anything."

"I agree with you, and I'm sure Lieutenant Rosen won't mind one teensy bit."

"Hang on and I'll check the sign-out sheet."

At this point, while I was on the edge of the stool and in danger of a topple, the door banged open and Gerald Galleston stalked across the room. "Just what do you think you're doing?"

I held up a finger. "Wait one second and then we can talk. I'm on hold for an important piece of information."

He took the receiver from my hand and replaced it. "No, we're going to talk right now. I don't know why you're meddling in my affairs, but I don't like it. Just what gives you the right to talk Maribeth into this job? She has no business working. She needs to stay home and take care of the house."

"It's only two hours a day," I said, gazing sadly at the telephone. "I need some help."

"Maribeth's hardly going to be of help," he said with a sneer. "She's likely to frighten away the customers. Furthermore, it's embarrassing to me for her to be seen in a store this close to campus, much less to be doing menial tasks. She was perfectly happy stuffing her mouth and watching television like a zombie. How'd you bully her into it?"

I gave myself a quick lecture on moderation, then managed a cool smile. "I asked her if she might enjoy getting out of the house for a few hours every day. You may think she's having a wonderful time in solitary confinement, ignoring her weight problem and allowing her brain to atrophy, but I don't. Once she loses a few pounds on this program, she'll—"

"What program?" he interrupted in a decidedly ominous voice.

Alas, if only life had a rewind button. "She's enrolled in a diet program," I admitted. "She'll be able to pay for it out of her salary."

He silently stared at me, his hands clenched into fists and his lips so tight they were almost invisible. I was about to inquire if he were in need of medical assistance when he said, "How much does this program cost?"

"Oh, it's hard to say. It depends on the length of the program. In any case, she signed a contract this afternoon, so she's committed to follow through on it. You ought to be pleased that she's making an effort to gain control of herself."

"Yeah," he said, "I'd be pleased if she looked less like an aircraft carrier, but no wife of mine is going to work outside the house. She can wait until the family fortune rolls over to her next year to do something about it. What's the name of this rip-off joint? She's not competent to scribble her name with a crayon, much less to sign a legally binding document."

"The Ultima Center," I said, wishing dear Joanie Powell were present to argue with the man. She'd gotten me into the mess, but she lacked the decency to be around when the excrement hit the fan.

Gerald turned on his heel and stalked back out the door without even thanking me for the information or waving good-bye. Then again, he was a member of the world's second oldest profession, which had certain parallels with the oldest. I waited until he'd cleared the portico and vanished, then picked up the receiver and called the CID again.

The gods had put down their pom-poms. I was told Peter would be with me in a second and was treated to a watered-down version of an old rock tune until he came on the line.

"I heard you were inquiring about me earlier," he said with an audible smirk. "I'm so sorry I wasn't in. What luck

I was back in time to take this call and thus save you the bother of tracking me down."

"I just wanted to invite you for dinner tomorrow."

"Of course you did."

I resisted the urge to play a round of did-too, did-not, and merely said, "Well? Can you escape this so-called major muddle for the evening, or has it become so consuming that you're obliged to exist on hamburgers and no sleep?"

"I think I can arrange a few hours for dinner and relaxation, although we may not get much sleep."

We settled a time and exchanged good-byes, he with his smirk and I with my sigh. No doubt he'd instructed the desk sergeant not to divulge his whereabouts in the future, thus thwarting the ploy. If Gerald the Bully hadn't come in at that precise moment, I would have at least learned the location of the investigation. With that knowledge, the follow-up would have been a piece of cake straight off someone's silver platter.

When I stopped on the porch to collect my mail, Joanie popped out of her apartment. "Why don't you come in for a drink to celebrate," she said.

"I'm not sure a dirge wouldn't be more appropriate," I said, then told her about Gerald's reaction to the idea of Maribeth doing anything other than vegetating. "I would imagine he convinced the Ultima people to tear up the contract," I concluded.

"But he didn't. Maribeth just called to say he was impressed with the program and very supportive. He doesn't object to her job either. It may have had something to do with the fact I told her the chancellor's daughter works for you every summer."

"She does?"

"I'm sure she would if you'd ask her," Joanie said with the self-complacency of a hyena hunkering down over a ripe carcass. "Shall we have that drink?"

I followed her into her apartment and accepted a well-earned glass of scotch. "I'm amazed Gerald changed his mind. He was rather strident about the matter only two hours ago, and firmly opposed to the entire scheme. He lathered and foamed at the very idea of Maribeth doing anything outside the house, and actually sounded alarmed at this change in the status quo. He almost acted as if he prefers her in her present condition so he can maintain control over her.''

"And over her inheritance," Joanie murmured. "He may be in for an unpleasant surprise."

"I certainly hope so," I said.

The next morning I was awakened not by my alarm clock but by an agonized shriek from the bathroom. Imagining all sorts of accidents involving wet tile or razor blades, I leapt out of bed and rushed to the door. There was no smear of blood, no unconscious body on the floor, no indication of pain and suffering. Caron stood in one corner, her back to me.

"What's wrong?" I demanded.

Her eyes wide with wonder, she looked over her shoulder and said, "I've gained two pounds."

"But your carotid artery is intact? Good grief, you almost gave me a heart attack with that imitation of a banshee. I thought you'd—"

"Two pounds," she said, dazed. "I cannot believe it. There's something wrong with the scales, Mother. There must be. Inez and I drank as much of that swill as we could choke down, and we're supposed to have *lost* between two and three pounds by now."

"Maybe it'll drop tomorrow," I said, heading for the kitchen to start the coffee. One needs to be fully caffeinated to deal effectively, or even ineffectively, with a fifteen-year-old.

"I've got to call Inez. This is a nightmare worse than anything that happens on Elm Street."

I got the coffee going and was heading for my bedroom when Caron stumbled out of hers and grabbed my arm. "Inez has gained three and a half pounds, Mother. What's happening to us? Is this some kind of cruel joke?

Did you and Inez's mother tinker with the scales or some-thing?''

"Of course not. Are you sure you're mixing up the proper ingredients in the blender and using the right amounts?''

"Absolutely. We've been switching back and forth be-tween the chocolate shake, which tastes like chalk, and the vanilla, which tastes like latex paint. Each serving has ex-actly three hundred calories.''

Aware that I would think more clearly in my bedroom slippers, I wiggled free and said, "I don't see how anyone could gain weight on nine hundred calories a day. You must be retaining water until your body adjusts to the re-gime.''

Caron's face turned as white as her bathrobe. "Nine hun-dred calories a day?'' she whispered.

"Three hundred times three. Don't worry about this weight gain; it's temporary, and in a day or two you'll lose all of it and a couple more pounds. Let me get my robe and slippers, then you can blend your breakfast while I inhale coffee.''

"Nine hundred calories a day?'' she repeated in the same stricken voice.

"You're taking algebra at school, but I presume you still remember some of the more basic computations. Would you like me to show you on a piece of paper?''

She clasped her hands to her mouth and darted back into her room. I put on my robe and slippers, ran my fingers through my hair (which was grayer than it had been five minutes earlier), and was at the kitchen table when Caron joined me.

"Inez and I goofed,'' she said, now subdued. "Neither one of us realized that we were supposed to drink that stuff instead of eating. We thought it was some miracle drink that made you burn calories, and we were having it between meals.''

She was so deflated I didn't have the heart to laugh, despite the temptation. Instead, I patted her hand and suggested she reread the book with a shade more attention to the overall diet plan.

"We agreed we can't drink any more of that stuff; it's enough to make a pig gag." Caron shot a quick look at the refrigerator, shrugged her shoulders, and said, "There's no point in starting another diet while we're both so depressed. Is there any sausage?"

FOUR

When Maribeth came in the next afternoon, I yielded to my curiosity and asked her why Gerald had changed his mind about both the part-time job and the Ultima program.

She shrugged. "I really don't know, but all of a sudden he's very much in favor of it. When he came home for lunch yesterday and I told him I was thinking about a part-time job here, he almost choked on an olive. I was . . . a little bit afraid, although he's never struck me or even raised his hand. His abuse is verbal, not physical." She hesitated, blinking rapidly. "But when he came home last night, he said he'd had a long talk with Candice and she'd persuaded him to allow me to try the Ultima program. She's very articulate, and I guess he was impressed."

"He came by yesterday afternoon, and he was more than a little vehement in his opposition," I said. "I'm surprised he was willing to listen to anything, much less a lengthy sales presentation."

"Candice can lay on the charm with a trowel. In any case, Gerald brought home some pamphlets about environmental cues, and has agreed to attend the weekly meetings for family members of those in the program. The first one's tonight."

"How were your first twenty-four hours on the program?"

"All I'm allowed are vitamins, potassium, liquid protein supplements, and ten glasses of water. I've been hungry enough to engage in auto-cannibalism, but it doesn't really bother me. I'm pretending that the gnawing pain in my stomach is a troll eating fat cells."

"Good for you. When do you start the exercise part of the program?"

"Today, after I weigh in. I dread this more than anything. I really don't want to put on a leotard and allow all those peppy, flat-bellied size threes to see my body. Even in sweats I'll feel like a great gray elephant, huffing and puffing through the jungle while they swing effortlessly through the treetops. However, Candice says it's terribly important to maintain a high metabolic rate, and she says this Jody is a great instructor. I wish I had a friend to come along for moral support, but I know hardly anyone in town." She gave me a look that indicated that she did happen to know someone in the immediate area.

"I don't sweat voluntarily," I said hastily, "but I'm sure Joanie will go with you this first time."

"She has a special class from four-thirty until six. But that's okay, Claire; I'll survive somehow, and I've got to stop behaving like a kid on the first day of school. I don't need someone to hold my hand when I cross the street.'

Maribeth gave me a smile, but I could see the panic radiating from her eyes like darts. I reminded myself of my ingrained aversion to strenuous physical activity that resulted in screaming muscles and damp, frizzy hair. I forced myself to envision both digits of my age—in neon, blinking like a digital clock. I wisely pondered what a twisted ligament could do to my mobility and thus my income.

"I'll go with you," I said with a sigh. "Caron and Inez come in at four; they can mind the store for a couple of hours. Do I truly have to wear a leotard?"

"Not the first time," Maribeth said, beaming at me.

I retreated to my office to see if somewhere in my chaotic

filing system I had a hair coat and a whip. Self-flagellation seemed to be the order of the day.

Joanie breezed in at four, but I told her I'd drive Maribeth to Ultima and stay with her for the exercise class afterward. Joanie patted my cheek and told me I was a good person. I resisted the urge to pat her fanny with my foot and told her she was a coward who needed more than a visit to a wizard to redeem herself. While she was formulating a reply, Caron and Inez appeared. I told them to stay until I returned, then hustled Maribeth out to my car. I stopped at my apartment to grab a T-shirt and a frayed pair of Caron's gym shorts, and we drove across the campus toward the diet place, the fitness center, and doom.

"Did you hear about that football player?" Maribeth asked idly. "Awful, wasn't it?"

I nearly ran into a pickup truck that capriciously had opted to stop at a stop sign. Once I'd caught my breath, I said, "Not a word, but I never read the sports section. What's happened? Was he murdered?"

"He had a heart attack in the middle of practice. He was running laps and then just turned blue and collapsed. The coaches tried CPR, but he was dead by the time the ambulance arrived. I think the article said he was twenty years old."

"Truly awful," I said, disappointed that I hadn't heard of some major muddle worthy of Peter's expertise. "One would think that the athletes are examined regularly to make sure they're in decent physical condition."

"Sometimes doctors miss things, especially if they don't know what they're looking for. This boy probably had a congenital problem, or permanent damage from a childhood disease."

I turned down the steep hill that led past Farber Stadium, home of the Fighting Frogs. The field was dotted with helmeted hulks in green shirts, all busily kicking footballs, chasing each other, knocking each other down, lunging into padded uprights, and basically engaging in various incomprehensible activities better known as practice. "Then they didn't call off the remainder of the season out of respect for the player who died?''

''I think that sort of thing happens quite a bit,'' Maribeth said, shaking her head as she looked down at the field. ''Some of the athletes get too involved in perfecting their bodies, while others of us break mirrors and dress in the dark.''

I couldn't think of anything to say, so we drove the rest of the way in silence. I parked under a shiny new sign that proclaimed in bold red letters ULTIMA DIET CENTER: WE DON'T WIN IF YOU DON'T LOSE. On the left was a slightly faded sign that said DELANO'S FITNESS CENTER.

Maribeth sat for a moment, then opened the car door and struggled to her feet. I followed her up the sidewalk and through a glass door with the daily schedule painted on it. Inside was a counter, on top of which was a silk flower arrangement and a clipboard, and beyond it a glass-enclosed office occupied by a petite blond-haired girl and a noticeably voluptuous black-haired woman in a tight white uniform. The two were discussing the contents of a manila folder, but they glanced up as the door closed behind us.

The blonde appeared to be no more than twenty. She had a dewy complexion that exuded innocence, in contrast to her thick lips and wide, heavily made-up eyes. She clapped her hands, and in a childishly high voice, said, ''Oh, Maribeth, I'm so happy you came back! This is so exciting!''

The other woman was less exuberant. Her hair was pinned neatly under her white nurse's cap, and her makeup was deftly muted. Smoky gray almond-shaped eyes gave her an obliquely oriental appearance, as did her olive skin. She was somewhat older than her companion, judging by the sprinkling of fine lines around her eyes and the softness below her chin. Despite the minor concessions to age, she might have stepped off the set of a television show, and I had no doubt she'd easily persuaded Gerald to allow Maribeth to enter the program. She could have talked him into lecturing on trade regulations in the nude.

Smiling warmly, she came to the counter and turned the clipboard around. ''Congratulations, Maribeth; I knew you'd decide to stick with the program. We'll work together to reach your goal, and when we do, you'll be a brand new person ready to take on the world.'' She raised a delicately drawn eyebrow at me. "Have you brought in your first referral? As I told you yesterday, you'll receive a free box of the protein supplement of your choice, or a twenty-dollar reduction in your permanent maintenance program.''

"I'm along for the ride,'' I said coolly. Sleekly. Unlike someone in need of a seven-hundred-dollar diet.

"Oh, of course,'' the woman said, laughing. "No one is allowed in the examination rooms with the client. If you'll wait in the reception area, I'll take Maribeth right back for our consultation. I'm sure you can find something to read in the rack.''

Once Maribeth had been whisked away, the blonde leaned over the counter. "There's really not much to read on the rack, unless you want to learn all about the perils of excess adipose and clogged arteries. Can I get you a diet soda or a cup of coffee? Maribeth's going to be a few minutes; Candice has to go over all sorts of details about the program.''

I agreed to coffee and declined artificial sweetener. After I'd been rewarded with a plastic cup of murky gray liquid, I asked the girl how long Ultima had been open.

"This is our first week, and it's so exciting! We've already signed up twelve clients. If you know someone who might want to sign up, I'm sure Dr. Winder will give you, you know, like a quiet little bonus for the referral. You certainly don't need protein supplements or an extra month of maintenance, do you?''

We both chuckled at the very idea. In that she was wearing a miniskirt and a hot pink T-shirt rather than pristine white, I asked her if she was a registered nurse.

"Goodness no! I'm just plain Bobbi Rodriquez, a junior at the college, majoring in physical education. After I graduate, I want to coach girls' basketball or maybe own a fitness center like the one next door. Right now I lead one class after I finish here, but I can't imagine anything more fun than leading aerobics classes all day, can you? I've already started building up my leotard wardrobe. I found this incredible spandex outfit during my lunch hour today. Would you like to see it?''

I was eroding rapidly, and we hadn't even started the exercise class. Before I could couch a refusal in polite terms, Bobbi bounced over to a filing cabinet, picked up a sack, and bounced back to show me her incredible spandex outfit, which to my jaded eye appeared to be a size one. Or zero. Or minus one.

''Don't you just love it?'' she demanded.

I admitted that I just loved it. I was about to be pressured into further lies when a man wearing a white coat over a pastel blue shirt entered the office through a door in the wall opposite the window. He reached toward a somewhat rounded part of Bobbi's anatomy, then spotted me and smoothly redirected his hand toward the desktop. ''Ah, very good, Bobbi, I was looking for Mrs. Galleston's folder. Did she bring in those old medical records?''

''Gee, I don't think she did, Dr. Winder,'' Bobbi said, giggling. ''Anyways, that's Mrs. Alawan's folder; Candice has Maribeth's. Do you want me to ask her now while she's with Candice, or shall I wait until she comes back out?''

''There's no rush,'' he said, then smiled at me. ''Do we have a new client? I'm Sheldon Winder, M.D. I'm the resident physician here at Ultima, available for consultation five days a week from nine until five and Thursday evenings until nine, because we feel our program requires close medical supervision, along with support from the staff and a commitment from our clients. And if you don't lose, we don't win.''

''She's a friend of Maribeth's,'' Bobbi hissed. ''She's not buying.''

''Well, then, we're delighted that you're giving her this kind of support, particularly during the first few days on the program,'' he murmured. He went out the far door, and then came through another into the reception room. He looked as if he were no more than a year or two out of medical school, although I knew that the required years of internship and residency meant he was more likely to be in his early thirties. He had clear brown eyes, stylishly cut hair, and a lopsided grin that contributed to his boyish demeanor. He wore brown-framed glasses, possibly in an attempt to make himself look older. Personally, I preferred the grandfatherly variety of doctor, who's had a few decades to perfect his art. After all, they do call it practice.

"How nice to meet you," I said, shaking his slightly damp hand. "Maribeth's quite enthusiastic about the program. I was afraid her husband, who's a lawyer, would demand the contract be torn up and the obligation canceled. I was pleased that you and your wife convinced him to allow her to continue."

Dr. Winder frowned at Bobbi. "Maribeth's husband was here? Why wasn't I informed of this? You know how strongly I believe in a family support system."

"He came in yesterday, just as I was locking up," she said, her cheeks turning pink. "You'd already gone off to that meeting at the hospital, but Candice was still here, so she took him back to her private office to explain the program and the details of the contract."

"And he didn't have any problems with the small print?" Winder continued.

Bobbi shook her head decisively. "He looked kind of scary when he first came in, like he wanted to beat somebody up, but Candice said she straightened him out in no time at all and sent him away with the environmental cues material."

Winder nodded, but before he could leap back into his diet jargon, the door opened and Maribeth joined us. Her voice almost shaking, she said, "Guess what—I lost three pounds! What's more, my blood pressure's down."

Winder threw his arms around her and hugged her as if she'd led the field in the Kentucky Derby. "That's absolutely marvelous, Maribeth! Fantastic!"

Bobbi looked a little misty as she said, "That's so exciting, Maribeth! You're doing just super."

Candice came to the doorway, a folder in her hand, and said, "Isn't this so thrilling for Maribeth, losing three pounds the very first day? Her ketones were right on the button, and when I read the scales, I was so breathless I almost had to sit down to collect myself.''

They all three looked at me. I realized some gush of enthusiasm was expected, hunted through my vocabulary for an adjective that hadn't been used, and finally said, ''That's wonderful progress the first day.''

Maribeth was given more praise, patted on the back, hugged, told repeatedly how successful she'd been, and sent out the door with a face reminiscent of a harvest moon. Once we were outside, however, she gave me a dry smile and said, ''They tend to get carried away with the positive reinforcement, don't they? I know perfectly well that the major part of those three pounds was water.''

''That doesn't matter,'' I said. ''You're going to stick to this diet, and pretty soon you'll notice the inches are disappearing, too. You'll look better and feel better and be a damn sight healthier. If it helps for the Ultima staff to stage a Broadway production every day, then why worry about it?''

''I did stick to the diet, didn't I?'' she said under her breath, then pointed at the sign above the fitness center. ''This class is supposed to be for beginners. It's low-level for the first few weeks, and the sessions only last forty minutes. Later, when we're in better shape, the sessions are an hour and a lot more demanding.''

The only positive thing I could think of was that I wouldn't be chaperoning her when all that happened. I muttered something and dutifully followed her through the door, nurturing vile visions of petite bodies shouting, ''Burn, baby, burn,'' and other encouraging remarks more appropriate to ghetto uprisings or weenie roasts.

The front room of the fitness center was large, decorated tastefully in yellow concrete blocks and a few posters of bug-eyed people contorting their bodies into gruesome bulges. The plants were plastic, as were the chairs scattered in the front of the room. There were two doors in the back, neither of which interested me. There was a short hallway on one side with several doors visible, none of which interested me.

There was an enormous mirror on the opposite wall, which appalled me. Sweating was unsavory; watching oneself sweat was unspeakable. As we hesitated, two young women appeared from the hallway and began to stretch in front of the mirror. A moment later, a white-haired woman joined them. All three had the trim bodies and grim visages of Rumanian gymnasts.

"I'm not sure what the procedure is," Maribeth said nervously. "I know I'm supposed to fill out a form, but I don't see anyone who appears to be in charge."

"One of those women might be Jody."

Neither one of us seemed inclined to ask, so we stayed by the door. The older woman stopped stretching long enough to put a cassette in a jam box. Violent rock music blared, and the three began to bobble furiously to the insistent rhythm.

"Maybe we ought to try again tomorrow," I suggested, inching backward with total disregard for the beat. "It looks as if the class has already started, and if this is a low-level class for beginners, I'm Jane Fonda."

Maribeth caught my elbow before I could bolt. "It's vital to the program that I participate in an exercise class three days a week. If I don't start now, I probably never will."

"Oh, all right," I said ungraciously. "Let's find Jody and get you enrolled." I went over to the older woman, who was flailing her arms and kicking her legs like a crazed Rockette, and said, "Where do we find Jody?"

She gave me a blank look and began to prance in place, her knees threatening her chin. I realized she hadn't heard me, and shouted, "Jody? Are you Jody?" The music stopped in the middle of my question, and my voice was considerably louder than necessary in the sudden stillness.

"I'm not deaf," the woman said as she blotted her forehead with a terry-cloth wristband. "Jody's in the office, through that door." She glanced at her companions. "Again, or the other side of the tape?"

I hurried to the office door and knocked before the music

again began to blare. Over the noise I thought I heard some-one respond, so I opened the door and entered the room.

Two men were standing behind a metal desk. One was short, wiry, and dark-haired, with an Italian look about him. He wore a baggy white T-shirt and equally baggy sweat pants. The other was an oversized teenager with pale shaggy hair, a bad complexion, and a sullen expression. It grew more sullen as we studied each other for an uncomfortable minute.

"I was told Jody was in here," I said at last.

"Who're you?" the dark-haired man demanded.

"I'm Claire Malloy. A friend of mine wants to enroll in an aerobics class; I came along to help her sign up. I'm sorry to have disturbed you. If you can tell me where to find Jody, I'll work out the details with her."

"Hang on," he said, then scowled at the kid. "I don't know how many times I got to say it, but it's my decision and I'm the guy what happens to own the place. I warned you two, three times not to horse around on the equipment. Don't show your ugly face around here anymore, Marcus. I'll prorate your fee and stick it in the mail."

The kid grunted and went out a door in the back of the office, slamming it behind him. The man came around the desk and held out his hand. "I'm Jody Delano, Claire. You goofed on account of how it sounds like a girl, no offense, and I heard about it all the time when I was growing up in the Bronx. Had to get my butt kicked a hundred times before I made my point." His hand, unlike Dr. Winder's, was dry and firm, and his grin was wry. "Technically speaking, I'm Joseph Delano, Jr.; I was tagged with Jody to minimize con-fusion with my father. It causes confusion elsewhere, I'm afraid. Now, where's your friend?"

We went back to the front room. During my interval in the office, several other women had joined Maribeth by the front door; to my relief, they were not of the svelte persua-sion. I was asked to sign a release form absolving Jody from any liability should he push me into permanent disability. Those who intended to join for the six-week session filled out questionnaires, contractual agreements, and the same release form. I was hoping we were through for the day, but Jody then suggested we change in the dressing room for our first introductory warm-up.

The ensuing forty minutes confirmed my theory that hell was overpopulated and new arrivals were being assigned certain punishments on earth. The so-called easy warm-up was somewhat similiar to transitional labor without medication, but not nearly as much fun. Jody led the class, shouting instructions, changing cassettes, and joking in an appalling display of enthusiasm. Although he was sweatless and breathing normally, the rest of us were dripping copiously and gasping by the time he told us how well we'd done and suggested a trip to the Jacuzzi, to be followed by a visit to the sauna.

I had no inner resources (such as breath or energy) with which to argue, and I followed the others to the next phase of hell on earth. The group obediently boiled in the Jacuzzi, baked in the sauna, then one by one drifted out to dress with trembling hands and flee.

Once we were alone, Maribeth said, "Jody's a great aerobics instructor, isn't he? He's got so much energy and he's so enthusiastic."

"Kamikaze pilots were enthusiastic, too, which is why you never bump into them on the street." I gave up on my frizzly hair and picked up my purse and a bundle of damp clothes. As we headed for the door, I said, "You looked terribly pale during the second half of the class, Maribeth. Are you sure you ought to exercise so vigorously?"

"I'm fine," she snapped. She shoved open the front door and marched toward the car, her shoulders squared and her head erect.

I walked slowly after her, puzzled by her abruptness. Her pinched expression conveyed quite clearly that she wanted no further discussion of her fitness, or lack thereof, and I could think of no good reason to insist. The Ultima Center had done a thorough examination and had recommended she participate in the exercise class.

As we started to pull away from the curb, Bobbi came out

of the diet center, waved at us as if she'd been adrift in a lifeboat for forty days, and turned back to lock the door. She then waved once again and disappeared into the fitness center, the latest acquisition for her leotard collection tucked under her arm.

"She wants to lead aerobics classes when she grows up," I said to Maribeth.

Maribeth groaned, as did I. Even that hurt.

My knees were wobbling so badly by the time we reached the Galleston-Farber mansion that I could barely push down the pedals. I told Maribeth I'd see her the next day, and somehow managed to drive down the hill and across town to my driveway. Realizing that it would be undignified to crawl, I staggered upstairs and flung my poor, sad body across the sofa.

I was still supine when Caron and Inez appeared. I opened one eye and said, "Did you lock all the doors at the store?"

"What is wrong with you?" Caron said. "You look like something the cat spit up on the rug. And why are my old gym shorts wadded up under the sofa?"

"You look awful," Inez added.

"I went to an aerobics class," I said, wincing at the memories that flooded me like scalding water.

"Why?" Caron said in a shocked voice.

"I can't remember. All I know is that death sounds charming. A hot bath sounds charming, too, but I can't make it to the bathtub. I couldn't even make it to the kitchen for a drink. For the first time in my life, I'm willing to admit the validity of the phrase 'half dead.' "

'Inez and I have begun an exercise program," Caron said as she flopped down on a chair and studied her fingernails. "We're going to walk miles and miles every single day— unless it's raining too hard. Right, Inez?"

"Oh, yes. Today after we locked the Book Depot, we walked all the way up Thurber Street to the corner of School Street, and then back."

I considered the corner in question for a moment. "I think we can rule out the insurance agency, the bicycle store, and the beauty parlor. Did this hike take you into the ice cream store?''

Caron sniffed. ''We may have gone inside, but we only had single scoops of sherbert, because everybody knows it's less fattening. Walking burns up zillions of calories, so we came out at least half a pound ahead. I think I'll weigh in right now. Come on, Inez; I'll bet we can already see a loss.''

The wail from the bathroom was enough to drive me to my feet and propel me to the liquor cabinet.

FIVE

Things calmed down over the next two weeks, although I had the unnerving sensation that I was cruising with Captain Ahab at the helm. Peter had gone jaunting with the feds, which is the entirety of what he'd told me over a bottle of burgundy. In that I'd gotten precisely nowhere regarding the major muddle, I wished him a lovely time playing footsies with the CIA, the DEA, the FBI, the IOU, the QED, or whatever combination of letters he preferred right through XYZ. He promised to bring me a bumper sticker and we left it at that.

Maribeth showed up every afternoon, battled the hordes of customers, and departed at four o'clock for her consultation at Ultima and her exercise class. Caron and Inez were working their way through every miracle diet known to civilization. They'd eaten grapefruit before every meal, swilled various liquids, gulped down pills guaranteed to make ugly fat melt away while they slept, purchased an exercise video and watched it twice, eaten nothing but protein, eaten everything but protein, and sworn off carbohydrates for life. None of these regimens had lasted more than twelve hours, mind you; they were all determined to be ''boring'' or ''disgusting" or "too tedious" or "playing havoc with my blood sugar level." Both had gained a few pounds, but I lacked the courage to inquire about a precise figure.

I was scowling over some paperwork when Joanie came into the store, dropped her purse on the invoice beneath my nose, and said, "Well? What do you think about Maribeth?"

"She's doing fine. We're so busy she's often reduced to dusting the racks or reading, but she hasn't complained. Since I'm not paying her salary, I've no reason to complain, either."

"That's not what I meant," Joanie said, unamused. "I'm talking about this new person who's emerging from that tent dress. Haven't you bothered to talk to her at all, Claire?"

"I say hello and ask how she's doing. She smiles and says she's doing great. I retreat to my office—which is the purported reason for her presence—and work on the tedious stuff. My checkbook balanced for the first time in six years, but I can see from your expression that you're not impressed. You're probably the kind of person who catches the bank's errors, aren't you?"

"I've found a few," she said, continuing to frown at me. "You really ought to take a look at this new Maribeth. She's changed enormously since her first day at Ultima. I'm terribly proud of my creation."

"You're not the one eating cooked squash and broiled fish. But you're right; I haven't stopped to talk to Maribeth." I glanced at my watch. "Aren't you supposed to be picking her up now? It's almost two o'clock."

"That's what I'm talking about. After the first few days she worked out an arrangement with Gerald, and now she takes him back to the campus after lunch and keeps the car the rest of the afternoon."

Joanie stopped as the topic of our conversation came into the store. As Joanie had asserted, there was indeed a noticeable change in Maribeth. Although she was hardly lean, she was clearly making progress on the Ultima diet. The tent dress had been replaced with a skirt and blouse that looked tidier. Her hair was still pulled back in a ponytail, but it was clean and shiny. She had attempted to disguise a minor patch of acne with liquid makeup and she was wearing an attractive shade of pink lipstick. Her shoes were polished.

"Hey," she called with more animation than I'd seen before, "don't stop talking about me unless you're saying catty things."

"I was saying nice things," Joanie said.

"And I was about to add some more," I said. "You're looking great, Maribeth. How much weight have you lost?"

"Sixteen pounds," she said with a giggle that reminded me of just plain Bobbi Rodriquez of spandex fame. She gave us a blank look, then shook herself and said, "Good grief, I've forgotten what I was going to say. Anyway, sixteen pounds thus far, and a goal of twenty by next Monday. If I make it, I'm going to treat myself to a haircut."

"What a good idea," Joanie said. "I haven't seen you since you started using the car in the afternoons. What do you do before you come here?"

I expected to hear her say she shopped, or went back home to catch a soap opera, or something equally innocuous. She did not. Instead, she turned bright red, shuffled her feet, and in general behaved like a teenager caught sneaking in/out of the house in the middle of the night.

"Oh, I don't—oh, nothing, really," she stammered. "I just—well, I've been going to the fitness center on some days, I guess, but I—nothing."

Joanie gave her a bewildered look. "You sound as though you spend the time robbing convenience stores or carrying on with a bearded man in a shabby motel room."

"Me?" Maribeth laughed unconvincingly. "I'm not quite ready to embark on a life of crime; a ski mask would hardly be an adequate disguise, would it? I'm going to wait until I've lost another thirty pounds and then try an armored car."

I laughed unconvincingly. "It's probably wiser. Did you graduate from the low-level aerobics class, or is this an extra session?"

"Is what an extra session?"

"You said a minute ago that you go to the fitness center

before coming here," I said gently, although I was as bewildered as Joanie, if not more so.

"I did?" When we merely looked at her, she gulped several times and said, "Oh, yes, of course I did. I'm still in the same class at five o'clock. With this much bulk, a few leaps and I'd crack my ankles. I go to the center to work out on the machines in the back room to tone my muscles. Jody developed the program for me."

"Jody?" Joanie echoed.

I explained that Jody was not only the aerobics teacher but also an instrument of the devil, who took perverse delight in making others sweat, gasp, turn interesting shades of plum and fuchsia, and suffer each and every second of forty minutes, and then insisted his victims simmer in scalding water and bake in the equivalent of a mobile home on an August afternoon.

"He sounds charming," Joanie said when I ran out of hyperbole. "I've never cared for petty tyrants—even the peppy ones."

"Jody's not like that," Maribeth said in a shocked voice. "Claire may not have enjoyed the class, but Jody's really very concerned about his students. After the second class, he suggested I work out three times a week on the machines. I told him I couldn't because I didn't have transportation, but he pointed out that the car just sits all day in Gerald's reserved parking space on campus. I haven't driven in years and I'd let my license expire, but I practiced in Jody's car. I passed all the tests to have my license renewed."

"And there's no problem about the cost of the additional sessions?" Joanie asked with the delicacy of a chainsaw.

"They're free. In exchange, I run errands for Jody, or stay in his office and answer the telephone while he's at lunch. She gave me a sudden piercing look. "Why are you staring at me like that? There's nothing wrong with running errands, is there?"

"Of course not," I said, surprised.

The intensity vanished as quickly as it had appeared. She gave us an impish grin and said, "Sometimes when I'm leaving to drop off packages or pick up supplies from the stationery store, Jody asks me to bring back a sandwich for him and we have a picnic. I can't eat with him, because of the program, but we talk and he's very sweet. I consider him a personal friend as well as my instructor. I don't care to hear him criticized like this.''

Joanie shot me a quick look. "My goodness, Maribeth, it sounds as if you have an adolescent crush on him. Since I'm the one who convinced you to enroll in Ultima and the exercise class, perhaps I'd better check him out. I don't want my protégée involved with someone whose intentions are not honorable.''

"Does Gerald know about this?'' I added lightly, or so I thought.

Maribeth gaped at us. "What're you talking about? Why would Gerald know anything? Has he been in here asking questions? What did you tell him?''

"I didn't tell him anything,'' I said. "He hasn't been in for two weeks, and I wouldn't know what to tell him if he did appear.'' I decided it would be wise to change the subject before Maribeth's eyes exploded all over the store. "Is he still attending the group support meetings?''

"He goes two or three times a week,'' she said, relaxing somewhat. "I think there's one tonight. He's been cooperative about the diet program. He used to buy bags of candy and potato chips, supposedly for himself, and then leave them on the counter to torment me. As you can see from this body, it always worked. He also insisted on fried foods and desserts at every meal. Now he doesn't bring anything illegal into the house, and doesn't complain about the broiled fish and steamed vegetables.''

"It sounds as if he's doing everything he can to help you,'' I said, wondering if I'd misjudged him.

Maribeth's explosion was verbal rather than optical, but almost as frightening. "He sure as hell ought to! After all the misery he's put me through over the last five years, the sleaze owes me something! He's damn lucky I haven't filed for divorce—and it's not too late! Mr. International Law might find himself working in some seedy office in Hong Kong, filing reports on obscure regulations, or cleaning the commodes.''

She stomped down the aisle. Seconds later the lavortory door slammed like a gunshot. Joanie and I looked at each other for a long while, then I shrugged and said, ''My goodness, that was quite a mood swing, wasn't it? We went from giggles and picnics to panic, fury, and divorce without any transition. What do you think came over her?''

''I have no idea,'' Joanie murmured. ''She was always a pleasant child, even in junior high. I've never seen her lose her temper, much less use even the mildest profanity. Do you think she might be ill? Her eyes seemed yellowish.''

''The diet could be responsible,'' I said, listening for the sound of the door opening. ''Her caloric intake on the Ultima program is not very much, especially in proportion to her body weight. Do you think you ought to speak to the staff there?''

''They went on at length about the fastidious medical supervision, how they monitor the urine samples and blood pressure and watch for any side effects from the program. Surely they'd adjust the diet if it were causing this kind of mood swing.''

''They may not have seen it,'' I pointed out. Before I could continue, a delivery boy carrying a long white box with a white ribbon came into the store. ''Mizz Gallton?''

''No, but we can produce a Mrs. Galleston,'' I said.

''Close enough,'' he said, handing a pad and pencil to Joanie. ''Sign there at the bottom.''

She did as requested. He put the box on the counter and left. The door at the far end of the room opened and Maribeth returned, now looking as placid as a cow in a field of clover.

I pointed at the box. ''This was delivered a minute ago.''

''For me?'' she gasped in the classic tradition. She untied the ribbon and pulled off the lid to expose long-stemmed roses in a bed of green tissue paper. ''Good heavens, who sent these?''

"There's the card," Joanie said, sounding as if she were very close to snatching it up herself.

Maribeth opened the envelope and pulled out the card. She read it, then stuffed it back in the envelope and dropped the envelope in the box.

"Well?" Joanie demanded. "I'm so itchy with curiosity that I can feel the bumps. Who sent these beautiful roses? Gerald? Is it your anniversary?"

A dark look crossed her face, and her voice was gruff as she said, "Yes, they're from Gerald. He's never sent me roses before, or even picked a dandelion and handed it to me. Now he's getting a little worried. After what he proposed last night, he should be." She looked at the roses, shook her head, and turned to me with an angelic smile. "Shall I change the window display? Some of the covers are faded."

I told her that a new display would be lovely, and Joanie left for an unspecified destination. As I started toward the office, I could hear Maribeth humming to herself as she gathered up the books in the window. I glanced at the box. The card glanced at me. If Joanie could feel bumps, I could feel welts the size of grapefruit. I nonchalantly went behind the counter and took out the notebooks in which orders were recorded, then delicately pinched the envelope from the box. The card said *Trust me.* A most peculiar anniversary message, I thought as I returned the envelope to the box.

At four o'clock Maribeth came to the office to tell me she was leaving, then did so, her expression still bovinely serene. Three minutes later Caron and Inez came in to announce that they were going on the seven-day rotation diet. They dropped a shopping list on the counter. I appeased them with a promise to read the list and dealt with a stout matron who wanted a book of quilt patterns, a book of counted cross-stitch designs, and, when Caron and Inez finally left, an exceptionally pornographic best seller.

At the appropriate hour I locked the door and started up Thurber Street, still worrying about Maribeth. I'd decided to stop at Joanie's, but as I came up the sidewalk I saw Gerald standing on the porch.

"Claire, I'm so glad I caught you," he said, thus destroying any idle hope that he was waiting for Joanie or stealing my mail or doing anything other than waiting for me.

Reminding myself that I might have misjudged him, I said, "Was there something you wanted to talk about?"

"Yes, but I think it might be more prudent to have this conversation in your apartment." He glanced at his watch. "I have an appointment in thirty minutes. Shall we get on with it?"

I decided I hadn't misjudged him. "By all means," I muttered. I took my mail and gestured for him to come upstairs. Once we were in the living room, I sat down and said, "I also have plans for the evening, Gerald, so let's indeed get on with it." I didn't elaborate, in that my plans involved an appointment with a steamy bath and a cozy mystery novel.

"Has Maribeth said anything to you about this Delano character?"

"She said he was an excellent aerobics instructor, that he had developed a program on some kind of muscle toning machine, that he was concerned about her general health."

Gerald went to the window and stared out for several minutes, his hands clutched behind his back. When he turned around, his face was grim. "I think this guy is trying to pull something. God knows Maribeth is insecure enough to fall for anyone who fawns over her, and that's what this Jody seems to be doing with his special program and that kind of crap."

"Maybe he's taking a genuine interest in her. Maybe he likes her."

Gerald's laugh was harshly incredulous. "Maribeth's mind is sophomoric, and the only thing that intrigues her is the plot of whichever idiotic soap opera she watches these days. She rarely reads a newspaper, much less any news or scientific magazine that might provide the basis of an intelligent exchange. She's shed a few pounds, but we haven't been disturbed by a sudden influx of admirers with flowers and champagne. I would imagine she's responsible for any lack of business you've experienced the last two weeks; there's a proven correlation between customer satisfaction and the physical appearance of the employees.''

''Business has been normal,'' I said, allowing an edge of hostility in my voice. ''Maribeth's not the slug you assume her to be. I happen to enjoy her company, although you obviously don't. That doesn't strike me as the basis of an intelligent marriage.''

He sat down beside me, several inches closer than I found comfortable. ''Now don't get me wrong. I must admit I feel sorry for her. When we were first married, she had a reasonable body and a functional mind. She wouldn't have lasted three days in one of my classes, but she was handling a less rigorous course load and making adequate grades. Art history is not the most challenging field; those with a degree are unsuited for any kind of employment except escorting schoolchildren around museums or lecturing groups of little old ladies.'' He crossed his legs and gave me a smile meant to imply neither of us would ever consider such a silly degree. ''But as I was saying, she wasn't all that bad seven years ago. I wasn't embarrassed to have colleagues to the house for wine and discussion, although Maribeth always hid in the bedroom with a bag of potato chips and a six-pack of soda. Over the last five years, however, she's deteriorated both mentally and physically, to the point I find it difficult to be with her, to be sexually aroused and find satisfaction. I'm sure you understand what I mean.''

I did, if only because he was leering so hard his eyebrows were likely to fall off his forehead. I moved away from him and said, ''Well, she's doing so well on the Ultima program that she may become her old self once again, and you can start inviting your colleagues over for wine and fascinating discussions of international regulations. I've noticed a remarkable change in her since she began the diet.''

''Have you? You're a very perceptive woman, Claire, as well as an intensely attractive one. How long have you been a widow?''

''Long enough to handle it quite well. Haven't you noticed a change in your wife? Joanie and I were commenting on it this afternoon. Maribeth seems much more animated, as though she's taking more of an interest in life. We thought it was a healthy sign.''

"Oh, she's animated, all right. She's also bouncing off the walls like a space cadet. She put a dent in my car the other day because she didn't realize it was in reverse. I've come home and found food charred in the oven because she didn't remember to turn it off. Hell, she's liable to burn the house down. It's to the point that I think it might be best to have her committed for a psychiatric evaluation and a nice quiet rest. The trustee may be a tightfisted old coot, but even he might agree she needs a legal guardian to arrange for treatment and handle her affairs until she's capable of doing it herself.''

"That's absurd,'' I said coldly. "The diet seems to have an effect on her moods, but surely it's temporary.'' As opposed to his guardianship and her confinement, both of which might be permanent.

"I can provide testimony that she was depressed before she started, and now she's showing signs of turning manic. I've got to leave now, but I do appreciate what interest you've shown in Maribeth. She needs friends who are intelligent, sensitive, and so very warm and womanly. If there's anything I can do to repay you, feel free to call—day or night.''

After another leer, he left me to ponder the question, is there one male on the planet who doesn't assume all single women are seething with sexual frustration and would therefore be eternally grateful for a romp on the mattress with absolutely anyone? A long question, true, but worthy of ponder.

Caron called to say that she was having dinner at Inez's house because Inez's mother (unlike certain Other People's Mothers) had bothered to pick up the items on the rotation diet and therefore provide a modicum of encouragement, along with a half cup of low-fat cottage cheese and green beans.

I suggested she convene a grand jury and have me indicted for maternal fraud, but agreed to run by the grocery store

and pick up whatever was needed for the seven days of rotation. I did not add that I would buy one-seventh of everything on the list. After I'd hung up, I glumly remembered
the list was at the Book Depot. I bribed myself with the
promise of a drink and an evening spent steaming through
the mystery novel, went downstairs and around the house to
the garage, and drove to the store.

I did all that was required to fetch the list, then continued
to the grocery store to buy minimal amounts of such goodies
as cottage cheese, green beans, beets, and tuna fish packed
in water. This particular diet had a life expectancy of one
more meal. As I returned to my car, it occurred to me that I
was in the vicinity of the Ultima Center and that Joanie Powell had not volunteered to discuss Maribeth's peculiar behavior with the staff. Maribeth had mentioned there was a family
support group meeting that evening, and Gerald had said he
had a six-thirty appointment. In a burst of deductive prowess, I decided the meeting was in progress and drove to the
center.

The lights were on in the office, but no one appeared after
I rapped on the locked door several times. It was obvious my
deductive prowess had failed me, I concluded, as I got back
in the car and dug through my purse for my key ring, which
had a tendency to burrow like a little mole into the deepest
corner. I was about to dump the damn contents on the seat
when the door of the fitness center opened and Maribeth and
Jody came out. I shamelessly slithered down until my nose
was even with the bottom of the car window and rolled down
the window a few inches.

"Doesn't he ever go out of town?" Jody said, his hand
toying with the back of her neck. "Once things are resolved,
I'd love to have one long, passionate, uninterrupted night
with you. We could spend an hour in the hot tub with a bottle
of champagne, then do all sorts of creative things in a bed
for hours and hours. I know exactly how to please a woman
like you . . . for hours and hours."

"Oh, Jody," Maribeth said in a breathless voice, "you
shouldn't say things like that. Someone might overhear you

and come to the wrong conclusion about our . . . friendship. Gerald would use it to prove how unstable I am and put me on the first bus to a sanitarium for a long, long rest. And no matter what you say, you're still in danger. You need to keep a low profile until they catch him.''

''Oh, baby, when they do, we're doing to have ourselves some kind of celebration.'' He put his other hand on the back of her head and kissed her for a long while. When he finally surfaced, his expression was smug. ''You're not crazy. You're a charmingly unpredictable woman what needs someone to love you and take care of you. You're blossoming, and I want to be the gardener who tends to you and nurtures every leaf and bud.''

It was pretty barfy, to use Caron's terminology, but Maribeth was buying every bit of it. Jody cooed some more botanical metaphors, gave her another long kiss, and walked her to her car. He stayed there until she drove away, and then he went back into the fitness center.

I was not pleased with the would-be gardener and his blossoming rose, but I reminded myself it was none of my business. I sat up, found my key ring, and was preparing to leave when I saw someone moving inside the Ultima office. Keeping the key ring in my hand, where I presumed I could find it when I needed it, I went to the door and knocked.

Sheldon Winder looked through the office window at me as if I'd popped out of a silver saucer. He mouthed something, but I shook my head and pointed at the locked door. After a moment of hesitation, he went through the door in the back of the office and came into the reception area, his brow creased and his eyes narrowed.

Feeling as if I had wobbly antennae, I managed a smile and again pointed at the door. When he'd unlocked it, albeit with reluctance, he mirrored my smile and said, ''We close at six o'clock. Perhaps you might come by in the morning?''

''I thought there was a family support meeting tonight,'' I said, stepping past him into the reception room. ''Maribeth seemed to believe her husband would be here, and although

I'm not a member of her family, I wanted to discuss her behavior these days."

"Tonight? No, I'm afraid you're mistaken. The family support group meets Wednesday afternoons at five. You're more than welcome to bring up this problem then."

He took off his glasses and meticulously cleaned them with his handkerchief. I suspected it was meant to imply that my visit was over and the door awaited me. Ignoring the message, I said, "This may not be appropriate for a group analysis, and I'd prefer to discuss her problems in private. As long as we're here, why don't we sit down for a moment and I'll explain what concerns me."

He settled his glasses back on his nose and pursed his lips. "That's not possible at this time." He stopped as we both heard a toilet flush in the back of the building. "I'm in the midst of a private physical examination with one of our morbidly obese clients who refused to come into the center during regular hours."

And I was in the midst of painting the ceiling of the Sistine Chapel.

"Dr. Winder,' I said in a low voice, "this will take only a few minutes, and I'm deeply concerned. Maribeth has invested over seven hundred dollars in the program in exchange for ongoing medical supervision, and now I believe she's having serious side effects that may endanger her health. Her husband may go to court to claim this diet has caused her to become mentally dysfunctional. Surely Ultima doesn't want bad publicity during its first few weeks of operation. Perhaps your client could read a magazine while we talk?"

His lips tightened briefly, then relaxed into a professional smile. "You're absolutely right, Mrs. Malloy. I'll go back to the client and ask her to wait; please make yourself comfortable and I'll be back shortly with Maribeth's chart."

He went through the door, closing it behind him, and after a moment murmured to the unseen client somewhere in the dark halls beyond the office. I studied the chart on the wall, which in unappetizing detail depicted all areas of the body that could build up slimy yellow deposits of nasty fat and then, according to the fine print, fail to function and result in disability and death. Mildly nauseous, I moved on to framed testimonials of those who'd lost fifty or ninety or more pounds and found a new purpose in life. They'd done so on the Ultima program and were forever indebted to the staff, to say the least. Some of us will read anything.

I was reading the business hours backward through the glass door when Dr. Winder reappeared, a folder in his hand, and brusquely asked me to sit beside him in the row of plastic chairs. He flipped through several pages, then said, "She's on the third stage of the program, an eight-hundred-calorie level, and is doing well. She takes a B complex and a multiple vitamin daily, along with three sustained-release potassium caplets of seventy-five milligrams each and four calcium tablets that total three thousand milligrams. In that the program is a protein-sparing modified fast, we insist the client include two to four protein supplements, which we offer in a variety of flavors. I devised the diet based on my extensive study of nutritional requirements, and I do happen to be a physician. She shouldn't experience any side effects from this."

"Well, she is," I said lamely.

"She may be going through some evolutionary changes due to her success on the program." He closed the folder and stood up. "I really must not delay my client in the back. If you wish further discussion, please come to the group support meeting on Wednesday. Candice will be pleased to explain what sorts of emotional upheavals may result in those who suddenly find themselves confronted with a brighter, thinner family member. I think you'll learn you aren't the first to feel a little bit jealous or resentful of a friend who's succeeding."

My eyes were still blinking and my jaw waggling as he escorted me to the door, held it open long enough to propel me out to the sidewalk, and locked it behind me with a loud click. Jealous and resentful of Maribeth's success? I finally found a suitably scathing remark, but as I turned back, the office light went out.

S I X

The following morning Peter wandered into the store, looking remarkably tanned for someone who'd supposedly been holed up with a bunch of spies. He cornered me between the travel guides and the cookbooks and spent several minutes greeting me with great skill. I felt like a devoted wife who'd been waiting for Hubby's return from the battlefield. Self-perceived Amazon warrior that I am, the image irritated me, although not enough to keep me from responding. And enjoying it.

"Did you miss me?" he murmured into my ear.

"Did you go somewhere?"

"Is that any way to get a bumper sticker?" He stepped back and pulled a folded rectangle from his pocket. "I thought you'd be overcome with emotion after our long and painful absence from each other's arms. However, I can see you're playing the role of a woman scorned, so I'll just give this to someone else."

"And allow my bumper to fall off in the driveway? I can see from your well-baked glow that the hush-hush guys didn't make you slave all day inside an igloo. Where'd you go—Hawaii or Key West?"

He flashed his teeth, which looked even whiter in contrast to his recently darkened complexion. "I was taking an all-expenses-paid crash course in one of the trendy new felonies. I can assure you that any sunbathing that occurred was not in the company of svelte nubile blondes but of fat manila folders of statistics. But I must confess there was a particularly sleek assault weapon that I couldn't keep my hands off. I can still feel that baby's hard metallic body as I cradled her in my arms. And those steamy sessions on the firing range, with the lingering aroma of spent shells, the rat-a-tat-tat of her sultry voice, the—"

"A trendy new felony?" I said, refusing to fall for a diversion of such magnitude that a parachute would be in order. "Anything that might tempt a mild-mannered bookseller?"

"I can't tell you, but I'm glad to see you've remained the same inquisitive Claire, the Miss Marple of Thurber Street. Should New Scotland Yard beckon you, we wouldn't want you to be delayed by a loose bumper." He held up the bumper sticker, which said DON'T DIET; LIVE-IT! "I thought Caron and Inez might be amused by this."

"Nothing amuses them anymore," I said, sighing. I listed all the disastrous diets that had been dismissed over the two-week period and admitted they had actually gained weight. "I had the audacity to suggest a sensible diet and exercise, but that was, of course, a waste of perfectly good carbon dioxide. They're determined to find a miracle diet that doesn't interfere with their daily regime of pizzas, cheeseburgers, and inertia. I think they're enjoying the investigation, but it's driving me to lengthy conversations with the bathroom mirror."

"How's your new clerk doing on her program?"

"Very well. As of yesterday, Maribeth's lost sixteen pounds, between the diet and the exercise classes. Her behavior is sort of peculiar, though, and I'm worried. I am not jealous."

"Why would you be jealous?" Peter said, leaning over the counter with a grin. "Are you worried that I might cast you aside when I catch a glimpse of this svelte, sweaty person?''

"Don't be absurd; you're much too old for her." I turned my back on him to gather up a pile of catalogues, then started for my office. "However, she ought to be here any minute, and she might find the bumper sticker so amusing that she swoons into your arms like a dying swan in a white tutu."

I took the catalogues to my office, dumped them on top of a stack of last season's catalogues, vowed that this would be the year I cleaned up the unholy mess, and went back to the front of the store in time to see Maribeth collapse into Peter's arms. "What'd you say to her?" I yelled as I ran toward them.

"Nothing. Help me lower her down gently, then get a cup of water and a damp washcloth."

I did as ordered, and within a minute Maribeth's eyes opened. "Where am I?" she asked, giving me a frantic look.

"On the floor of the Book Depot. You fainted," I said. I draped the washcloth on her forehead and helped her take a sip of water. "Stay here until you feel capable of walking, and then we'll take you back to the office to rest. When you're ready, we'll figure out how to get you and your car home."

"I'm better. Really." She pushed the cloth aside and sat up, her face puckered with anxiety and her hands fluttering in the air. "I would like to sit in the office, but just for a minute, and then I'll start work." She gave Peter a quizzical look. "Haven't I seen you somewhere before? Are you one of Gerald's colleagues?"

"Gerald's her husband," I explained. "He teaches at the law school."

"I'm Peter Rosen. I don't have any connections with the law school, and I don't remember meeting either you or your husband. Are you feeling steadier? Let Claire and me help you to the office."

As we guided her down the aisle, I said, "What happened, Maribeth? Did you feel dizzy?"

She stopped to think, then put her hands on her face and mumbled, "Yes, I felt a little dizzy. That's all. I'll be fine in a few minutes. Please don't make a fuss over this, Claire—

and please don't say anything to Joanie. She'll go screeching to the Ultima staff, and they'll refund my money and throw me out of the program. Jody'll be scared to allow me to participate in the aerobics class. This was my fault. I'm required to take potassium caplets three times a day, but yesterday was hectic and I missed a couple of doses. If you and Mr. Rosen agree not to tell anyone about this stupid dizzy spell, I'll swear I'll never miss another one.''

She was most likely correct in her predictions of what Joanie, the Ultima owners, and Jody would do if they suspected there was any chance that Maribeth was unfit and therefore posed a threat both to their reputations and their liability premiums. I gazed at Peter. "If you're certain that a potassium deficiency is responsible—and if you swear you won't miss another dose—I won't mention this," I said sternly.

"It's my only chance to break out of this horrid body," she said to Peter, clutching his arm desperately enough to endanger the Italian silk. "It's my last chance."

After we'd let her sink down in the chair behind the desk, he continued to look soberly at her. "I don't know any of the people, so I'm not in a position to speak to any of them," he told her. "I do think you ought to be checked by your private physician to make sure you're in shape for this diet and exercise class." When I nodded in support, he added, "Why don't you tell us his or her name, and Claire can make an appointment right now?"

"I don't have a doctor in Farberville, unless it's Dr. Winder. When I lived here as a child, my pediatrician was old enough to have written a chapter of the Bible. He's either retired to Florida or is in the cemetery by now, and in any case, I'd feel foolish sitting in a waiting room filled with comic books, little cars, and spotty babies. I haven't had any reason to use another doctor since we returned."

It made sense, but it came out in such a tumble that I didn't quite believe her, although I wasn't sure which bit of the story seemed iffy. "You're a little old for a pediatrician," I murmured, "but you do need an examination. How about my doctor?"

"I'm fine now! Just leave me alone!" she said belligerently, then hid her face with her hands and began to cry.

"We're going, we're going," Peter said. He took my arm and led me out of the office. When we were in the front of the store, and presumably out of earshot, he said, "Could she be on drugs?"

"Vitamins, potassium, calcium, that sort of thing. She's examined daily by a registered nurse, who monitors a urine sample and watches for bizarre behavior. If Maribeth were taking some unauthorized drug, wouldn't it show up in a urinalysis?"

"It depends," he said, frowning over my shoulder.

"What happened? Did she take a look at your moderately handsome face and pass out in ecstasy?"

"If she did, it's a first for all of us." He seemed to realize he was still frowning, and gave me a smile that went a full half-centimeter deep. "I said hello and showed her the bumper sticker. She stopped in mid-step and goggled at me as if I were showing her a piece of underwear I'd lifted from her lingerie drawer, put her hand on her chest, and crumpled down for the count. I didn't think the bumper sticker was all that funny, but we both know I've got lousy taste."

We both knew he didn't, especially in his choice of women. We discussed the scene for a while, and I agreed to try once again to persuade Maribeth to consult my physician, who happened to be an ob-gyn. Better than a pediatrician. At least the waiting room had back issues of *Cosmopolitan* and *Newsweek*, and the only babies present were in utero.

"Is it possible," I said as Peter started to leave, "that you could run a check on Sheldon and Candice Winder? Background, medical training, whatever. I'd feel more comfortable if I knew they were both what they claim to be."

"As in bogus credentials?"

"Dr. Winder recites diet jargon quite glibly, but he didn't seem to be the least bit concerned with Maribeth's symptoms and agreed to talk to me only when I mentioned a possible lawsuit. Then again, maybe I'm as flaky as Maribeth,'' I said, shrugging.

''But you wear it so well. I'll tell Jorgeson to see what he can find out, but it may take a few days.'' He gave me a chaste kiss on the cheek and left.

A few minute later Maribeth came out of the office, still wan but determined to work, and although I wanted to send her home, I left her to clean out the drawers below the cash register. She was, after all, nearly thirty years old and heir to a large fortune. She was entitled to swoon, rage, and contemplate an illicit affair with her aerobics instructor, all without my solicitous intervention. On the other hand, I told myself as I shoved aside the stack of catalogues, I might attend the family support group that afternoon, convince Candice that my motives were pure, and find out why the hell Maribeth was behaving as erratically as a punch-drunk boxer with oatmeal for brains.

Maribeth and I were doing an inventory of the science fiction paperbacks when Joanie came into the store. She studied Maribeth. ''How are you today, dear?'' she asked.

''I'm fine, and I wish everyone would stay off my case and stop clucking over me. I'm the one who's chosen to be on this program, and I'm more than capable of taking care of myself.''

''Of course you are,'' Joanie said soothingly. After an uncomfortable moment of silence, she said, ''Isn't this news about the football player distressing? According to the news on the radio, the athletic department's in quite an uproar—as well it should be. The poor boy was twenty years old. Such a waste.''

''Are you talking about the football player who had a heart attack several weeks ago?'' I asked as I jotted a note to myself about the fantasies, which were moving like salted slugs. Rack space being at a premium, we needed more carnivorous aliens and fewer dwarfs and cute little fairies.

Caron and Inez burst in before Joanie could continue. Caron pointed her finger at me and said, ''We've finally found the perfect diet, and it's one we'll be able to stick to for weeks

and weeks. It's based on eating fiber in order to make yourself feel full, so you're able to resist temptations."

Inez nodded. "It's very easy to follow, Mrs. Malloy."

"What's it called?" I asked, resigned to look pleased with
whatever I heard.

"The popcorn and grapefruit juice diet," Caron said.
"That's all you have, but you can have all you want of those
two things."

I fought back a wince. "It doesn't sound very appetizing.
Are you sure you can stick to it, Caron? You don't like grapefruit juice. In fact, I seem to remember that you detest it."

"That's the beauty of the diet. I like popcorn, and I loathe
grapefruit juice, so I won't be tempted to drink too much of
it. According to Rhonda, I can lose as much as ten pounds a
week."

"Rhonda's now an authority on nutrition?"

Inez blinked solemnly. "No, but her cousin in St. Louis
went on this diet and lost twelve pounds practically over-
night. Rhonda said it was like a miracle or something, and
her cousin wasn't ever hungry."

At least it was less expensive than tuna packed in water or
the dreaded seaweed regime. I chewed my lip. "You two
might discuss diets with Maribeth," I told them. "She's lost
sixteen pounds, and she's done so while eating fairly normally."

"Seventeen and one-quarter," Maribeth said cheerfully.
"By this afternoon, maybe eighteen."

Caron and Inez exchanged enigmatic looks. Caron folded
her arms and said, "Which one are you on?"

"It's basically well-balanced low-calorie meals with vitamin and protein supplements. I also go to aerobics classes
and work out on the toning machines, but that's the fun part,
and I look forward to my classes."

Joanie beamed at her. "And I must say that I'm terribly,
terribly proud of you, Maribeth. I wrote a letter to my daughter to tell her what progress you've made."

Caron and Inez again exchanged looks, but enigma was
replaced with wariness.

"How long have you been on this?" Caron asked in a challenging voice.

"Almost three weeks," Maribeth answered uneasily, clearly taken aback by Caron's demeanor.

Caron snorted. "I figured as much. This popcorn and grapefruit diet is much faster, and it doesn't involve any exercise. Why, in three weeks we could lose as much as thirty pounds, although naturally I'll only need one week and Inez . . ." She stopped and coolly appraised her cohort. "No more than two weeks, max."

"I don't need to lose twenty pounds!" Inez said, allowing a rare tinge of outrage to creep into her usually monotonal pronouncements.

"It couldn't hurt."

"You're the one they refer to as Miss Thunder Thighs."

"It's not my fault you have gym class third period, Pudgy-Wudgy. If moronic Louis Wilderberry had seen you thudding under the volleyball net like a hippopotamus—well, who knows what he might have thought."

"Louis Wilderberry can't tie his shoes without reading the directions."

To everyone else's relief, the two departed, the sound of their bickering wafting after them like a mist of acid rain. Once they'd cleared the portico, I sighed and said, "Please forgive them, Maribeth. After all their miracle diets, they've put on pounds. I heard Caron telling one of her friends on the telephone that she couldn't find any new jeans in her size that weren't too tight. If you think I suggested a bigger size, you seriously underestimate my will to live."

"I hope they don't resort to any diet pills," Joanie said. She gazed sternly at Maribeth. "And I assume you wouldn't even consider them. They're addictive and dangerous."

Maribeth stared at her, the blotches on her face beginning to throb angrily. Before she could sputter a response, I said, "We're done with this rack, Maribeth. Will you please use the calculator in my office to add up all the columns? I'm planning to call in an order tomorrow morning and I need the totals."

"All right," she said. She snatched the clipboard from my hand and stalked toward the office.

"I simply don't know what's happening to her," Joanie said, scowling at me as if I'd throbbed and sputtered and snatched and stalked. "Maybe we should speak to Dr. Winder or Candice."

"There's a family support meeting today at five," I said helpfully.

"What a pity. I'm having dinner with a girl from my pottery class, and then we're going to a lecture on Japanese firing techniques at the school. The lecture's at seven, so there's no way I can make it to this meeting. Poor Maribeth seems to be degenerating at an alarming rate; by next week she may be in serious trouble and beyond any help we might give her." Her sharp look made it clear who would be responsible should that happen.

"You started this," I protested. "You're the one who's the producer and director of the show, but every time someone needs to do something, you conveniently remember a previous engagement."

"Just look at the time! If I don't get the chicken in the oven, Violet and I will be late for the lecture. Tashimo Kokata is one of the best Japanese potters of the decade."

I realized I was outmanuevered once again and ungraciously wished her rubbery chicken for dinner and terminal tedium at the lecture. After she left, I picked up the newspaper and sat down behind the counter to see what the local citizenry had done for my amusement. I recalled Joanie's remarks concerning the dead athlete and turned to the sports page—a first in my present lifetime.

It was well worth the adventure into the unknown. The football player, Greg Smollenski, a sophomore from some small town in Kentucky and a brilliant linebacker (whatever that was) had indeed died from an acute myocardial infarction, better known as a heart attack. An autopsy, however, had indicated the boy had been using—or more accurately, abusing—anabolic steroids and corticosterioids for several months. The former I'd read about and knew were taken to increase muscle mass and strength, frequently resulting in heart problems and other unpleasant complications. The latter, according to the article, were used to increase aggression and mask pain and fatigue while busily causing gland dysfunctions that led to kidney problems. Neither was legal. Both were common.

The NCAA was not happy with the deceased player or with the Farber College Athletic Department, which was required to randomly test its athletes for signs of abuse. I ordered myself not to envision rows of brutish hulks clutching little bottles in their oversized paws and continued through the article. The football coaches swore they had no idea where the Smollenski boy had obtained the drugs, and muttered about ways to avoid detection in tests. The basketball coaches said there was none of that going on among their players. The wrestling coach had gone out of town indefinitely. The head of the department had played misty at the press conference and bemoaned the loss of such a fine, upstanding, Christian athlete with such golden opportunities ahead of him. His plea for a thorough investigation to put an end to such abuse among the fine, upstanding, Christian boys who gave their personal best for the Fighting Frogs had reduced the author of the article to tears, or so he claimed.

The final paragraph noted that the DEA and the NCAA were assisting the Farberville CID in the investigation.

Despite the unsavoriness of the story, I must admit I was grinning just a bit. Ol' Super Cop had almost been right when he smirkingly said that I'd never read about his case, not because it was hush-hush, but because he knew I never so much as glanced at the sports page.

The grin was still in place when Maribeth came out of the office and gave me the clipboard, saying, "I'm sorry I was so sensitive earlier, Claire. This program is so totally vital to me, and I don't want Joanie to do something that might result in my being sent back to that dreary house to do nothing but stare at the walls and stuff my face. It's done wonders for me, both physically and emotionally. I can almost believe someone might like me . . . or even love me. Once I gain control of the trust, I might go back east to finish my degree, and after that, use some of the capital to open a small art gallery somewhere.''

''With Gerald?'' I asked quietly.

''He's a loser. For years he's been convincing me that I was the loser, that I was fat and stupid and boring and unworthy of friends. All of a sudden he's become solicitous and attentive; last night he said he had a long conference with Candice about what he calls my 'mood exaggerations.' He brought me an extra bottle of potassium-caplets.''

''Which I hope you'll take.''

''Oh, I'll admit I've been a little giddy, but it's not from any organic imbalance. Gerald tried to tell me I was going through a predictable stage and would change my mind, but I assured him that the only thing I was going through was a divorce. There are men who might someday love me.''

I suspected she had a candidate in mind, and I could only hope she wasn't too desperate to remember she was soon to be a rich young woman with battered self-esteem. ''I'm sure there are lots of men,'' I said, stressing quantity.

''Your friend seemed nice,'' she said. ''He's very attractive.''

''And due for a surprise.''

She gave me a coy smile and left for the Ultima Center and her session with the sadist in the adjoining facility. I sat and debated with myself for thirty minutes, then grimly drove to the center for the family group. Young love might be the root of Maribeth's mood swings, or exaggerations, as Gerald as quaintly called them, but fainting was an acceptable side effect only in Gothic romances, where it was more the order of the day.

As I parked, Bobbi Rodriquez came out of Ultima and stopped beside me. ''Ooh, this is so exciting!'' she squealed.

''That I can park without assistance?''

''Just that you're here. Did you come for the group, or for an aerobics class? Jody said you didn't seem to enjoy the one you went to a couple of weeks ago.'' She tilted her head and put a finger on her cheek. ''You're not in bad shape for your age," she continued, fluttering her eyelashes at me. "I bet you were bored with the beginners' class; it's so incredibly easy that it's not very challenging. Do you want to try one of my classes? You can come once for free, and I promise we'll just work out until we're ready to drop right there on the floor."

"It sounds wonderful, but perhaps some other time."

"It is some other time," she said, fluttering harder. "It's at seven on Mondays, Wednesdays, and Fridays. Oooh, here's my ride. I'll be so excited if you come tonight, or another night, if you're busy as a bee." She waggled her fingers at me and scampered over to a rusty red sports car, which was, I noticed without interest, driven by the sullen boy I'd encountered in Jody's office. He glowered briefly in my direction, then pulled out of the lot in a spew of gravel, barely missing a station wagon and a pair of pudgy pedestrians.

I went across the sidewalk to the glass door, relieved that I did not have to produce an alibi for the evening. The pudgy pedestrians crowded behind me, and after a few awkward moments in the doorway, squeezed past me and headed down the corridor. They looked as if they might be related to an Ultima client, and for lack of anything better to do, I trailed after them, peeking curiously into small dark examination rooms with professional scales and padded tables covered with pristine white paper.

A larger room at the end of the corridor was lit. Half a dozen people sat on folding chairs, and Candice was serving coffee on a tray. Gerald was not there, but by this point I wasn't overcome with surprise.

Candice gave me a warm smile. "How considerate of you to come to help Maribeth. She's doing so well, and I think, despite these minor setbacks, that she'll reach her goal "

"Edwina sure won't," opined an elderly woman who weighed no more than seventy pounds and whose feet dangled several inches above the carpet. "Edwina thinks she's foolin' me, but she ain't. I hear the icebox door a-openin' every night 'long about midnight. She tries to open it real slow and sneaky so I won't hear it, but it squeaks like a hog gettin' castrated every time.''

The discussion went downhill from this point. Each of the members of the group had a long, involved personal anecdote about his or her beloved dieter and was encouraged to ramble on in considerable detail. Candice listened to all of them, making reassuring remarks and suggestions about how best to handle—in a supportive and nonjudgmental way, of course—the midnight prowlers, closet chocoholics, and other miscreants who were straying off the straight and narrow (a.k.a. eight-hundred-calorie) path. The two pudgy pedestrians both turned out to be clients, and we listened forever while they accused each other of unspeakable sins against the program. When my turn came, I considered relating each and every detail of Caron and Inez's fight against the flab but thought better of it and wanly gestured to the next speaker.

At five forty-five Candice stood up and congratulated us on our deep commitment to our family members and friends fighting the battle of the bulge. Everyone laughed politely and departed, chattering like kindergartners on a field trip. I waited until the last was halfway down the corridor, then said to Candice, ''As I told your husband last night, I'm concerned about Maribeth's behavior, especially in the last few days. At times she's vague, and then she abruptly flies into a rage. Today she fainted in the bookstore, although she claimed it was due to missing two potassium caplets yesterday.''

I expected a bit more than a raised eyebrow, but I was expecting in vain. ''You spoke to my husband last night?'' she said with a small laugh. ''And how could you have done that?''

''I knocked on the door and he unlocked it, although he was in the middle of a physical examination. He looked through Maribeth's chart and said the supplements were adequate. I wasn't convinced, and after today's episode I'm even more concerned.''

She went to the coffeepot in the corner and turned it off, then loaded the tray with plastic cups and other paraphernalia. Turning back, she said, "I've noticed a few unusual reactions from Maribeth, and I suggested that she increase her potassium and add an extra protein supplement or two daily. However, I think we must all try to ignore these minor outbursts and encourage her to stick with the program. I'm worried that her obesity might lead to serious systemic problems, and I know Gerald shares my concern. He's promised to monitor her very closely."

"Then you think she'll be able to remain on the program?" I persisted. "What about this bout of dizziness?"

"Our records are highly confidential, but since you're her closest friend, I'll try to explain what may have occurred. As I mentioned earlier, she's been forced to deal with several setbacks recently. Nothing of significance, but a stray pound popping back on when she claims to have stayed legal. She and I both know she's telling little white lies to cover up her indiscretions, but she refuses to admit it. This kind of denial can lead to a great deal of inner turmoil, and it's not uncommon for someone under that kind of pressure to feel a bit unsteady on her feet. I'll make a note of this incident on her chart, however, and try to help her face the reality that we all can slip at times."

"Setbacks?" I echoed. "She's never mentioned that."

"But she wouldn't, would she? Thanks again for coming by." Candice smiled at me and went out of the room.

I walked slowly down the corridor and through the reception room to the door. I'd never been intently involved in a diet that I perceived would change my life, but I couldn't understand how Candice's version of denial and inner turmoil could lay anyone out cold on the floor. As I opened the car door, Maribeth came out of the fitness center, a canvas bag in her hand and a strange expression on her face.

"What are you doing here?" she asked in an unfriendly voice.

I was too numbed from the meeting to concoct a clever lie, so I told her I'd come to the group to ask Candice about the fainting spell.

"Was Gerald there?"

When I mutely shook my head, she clasped the bag to her chest as if she could find warmth from it. Her face was white, as were her lips. The only hint of color came from the angry patches of acne on her chin and around her mouth. "No big deal," she mumbled, staring at the sidewalk. Her fingers tightened around the bag. When she lifted her head, there was a heretofore unseen expression on her face. It made me think of a defenseless animal treed by a pack of baying hounds.

"Maribeth," I began cautiously, "are you—"

"Your friend who was in the bookstore this afternoon's a detective, isn't he?"

"Peter? Yes, he's with the local CID. Why don't you let me give you a ride home? You can come back for the car later."

"Why was he following me? Doesn't he know what's going on?"

"He wasn't following you. We've been seeing each other for a quite a long while, and he came by to say hello after a trip out of town. Why would he follow you?"

"I don't know. You're right—there's no reason for him to follow me. It's too confusing, or maybe I'm just too dumb to understand. He keeps telling me to trust him, you know."

"Gerald's still insisting you consider a week or two of rest to . . . ah, relax and feel more in control of yourself?" It wasn't especially tactful, but it was the best I could do. "Would that be so bad?"

"I thought you of all people would be the one who understood, Claire. We're in the same boat, aren't we?"

"Which boat is that, Maribeth?" I asked in the same cautious voice, intently aware of how very near the edge she was.

"Don't you know? Aren't you worried?"

She certainly had part of it right. I took a breath, wishing I'd paid more attention in psychology classes two decades ago, and said, "All I know is that I'm very worried about you. Why don't we get in my car and discuss this further?"

She stared wildly at me, then swung around and climbed

into her car. The engine roared and she screeched into reverse, ground the gears, and raced out of the parking lot as
rapidly as the red sports car had done an hour earlier. I stood
where I was, thoroughly stunned, trying to think how best
to stop her before she crashed into a truck or wrapped the
car around a utility pole.

I let out my breath as her car braked at the stoplight. When
the light turned green, however, the car remained in the same
spot, the brake lights shining like red, demonic eyes. A car
behind Maribeth honked, but was finally forced to pull
around her, as were the next two in line. I was about to run
to the corner when the brake lights went off and the car began
to back up in a series of angular swerves and squeals until it
reached the edge of the parking lot. It manuevered around
until it was aimed in my direction; headlights blinded me as
it began to lurch forward.

Straight at me.

"What's going on?" Candice called from the doorway
behind me.

"I—don't—know," I croaked. I moved across the sidewalk to the Ultima door. "It's Maribeth. I don't know what
she's doing, but I don't care for it."

"Is she all right?"

"How the hell should I know? I think we might step inside, though." I shoved Candice backward and followed her,
all the while watching Maribeth's car as it lurched toward us,
the sound of the engine erupting like a warped record.

"Is she upset?"

"To put it mildly. Maybe you'd better call someone."

"Who?"

I spun around and gave her an exasperated look. "I don't
know—you're the owner of this place, the registered nurse,
the professional who said Maribeth was having a tiny problem with denial. I suspect she's in the midst of flipping out,
but I'm only a civilian." I was about to continue when there
was a deafening crash behind me. Shards of glass went flying
past me on all sides, and something stung me in the back. It

felt, I told myself with a hazy smile as my knees folded, like a giant bumblebee.

It was my last thought for the moment.

SEVEN

"**S**hhh," someone whispered, not too far from my ear.

I dearly hoped that the shush would have some effect on the ear in question, which was ringing like a fire alarm. Odd, I mused, that no one was urging me to exit the building in an orderly fashion and line up at the end of the playground so that roll call could be taken. Perhaps I was a monitor. . . .

I opened one eye to see if Miss Wornewood, my sixth-grade teacher, was hovering nearby with her black attendance book and her typically harried expression.

Joanie Powell looked more harried than Miss Wornewood ever had, including the month some of the boys had dedicated themselves to filling her (Miss Wornewood's, not Joanie's) desk with various reptiles and amphibians. "You're awake," she said (Joanie, not Miss W.). "How do you feel?"

I closed my eye to consider the question. After a moment, I determined that I felt as if I'd been run down by a motorcycle gang. "Lovely," I muttered. "Where am I, and where's Miss Wornewood?"

"The doctor said she might be groggy from the pain medication," Joanie explained in a satisfied voice.

By this time I'd figured out that I was lying in a bed, that my back was most likely a canvas of tread marks, that my buttocks had been used for a dartboard, and that the fire alarm was not going to cease its deafening din, no matter whether I exited the building or checked the girls' bathrooms for loiterers. A hand brushed my cheek, and I opted to try the other eye.

Peter looked pretty damn harried, too. "Claire? Do you understand where you are?"

"Shall I find the doctor?" Joanie said.

"Everybody calm down," I said. "I feel absolutely terrible, and my head may explode any second now, but the last thing I need is a doctor." I got both eyes open. The walls confining me were a revolting shade of green, the bed had rails, and stuck in my arm was a needle connected to a tube that ran up to a glass bottle on a stand. I clearly had had need of a doctor in the recent past. "If someone would be so kind as to explain . . ."

Peter bent over to kiss my forehead. "You were at the Ultima Center, remember?" he said. "For reasons we don't yet understand, Maribeth Galleston drove her car into the front of the building. A brick bounced off your lovely cranium, and a good-sized piece of glass went into your back, although it missed everything of significance. A lot of smaller ones caught you below the waist. The glass has been removed, and a great deal of pain medication is now dripping into your veins."

"Do you have any idea why Maribeth did what she did?" Joanie asked.

When I turned my head to look at her, a lightning bolt leapt between my temples. "Why don't the two of you pick one side of the bed?" I groped around in my remaining gray matter. "No, I don't know why Maribeth did it. I went to the family support group, survived forty-five minutes of platitudinous enthusiasm, talked to Candice, and then met Maribeth coming out of the fitness center."

"And?" Peter said encouragingly.

"And I suppose we must have talked, although the details are foggy. Or was it Bobby Spandex? Lord, I don't know.

Could someone please ask Miss Wornewood to turn off that damn bell?''

"She's delirious," Joanie announced.

"I am not delirious, nor am I deaf—although it's a matter of time," I said, grimacing. "If you'll give me a minute, I'll try to—what about Maribeth? Is she all right? And Candice? She was facing the door when everything came at us. Is she . . . all right, too?"

"Maribeth's in intensive care," Peter said gently. "I'm afraid Candice took a lot of glass in her chest area. Both lungs were punctured, as was her carotid artery, and she was pronounced dead at the scene."

"How bad is Maribeth?" I whispered.

Joanie patted my hand. "She's critical. She took a hard knock on the head when she slammed against the steering wheel. They did some tests and discovered she'd had a heart attack, either just before the accident, or as a result of the impact. She's in a coma. They're doing some kind of scan now to determine if there's irreversible brain damage. I feel like all this is my fault. I feel . . . dreadful." She moved away from the bed and sank down in a chair, clearly struggling to maintain her composure.

"I'll let you know about Maribeth's condition as soon as I hear from the doctor," Peter said. "Please try to remember what happened, Claire. We have no idea whether we're looking at an accident induced by a heart attack or some crazy attempted homicide."

"How long was I unconscious? And what about Caron? Did someone let her know what happened?"

"I called her as soon as I heard what had happened and let her know you were going to be okay. She can stay at Inez's house for a day or two while you're here at the hospital. You were out for almost twelve hours; it's not quite daybreak yet. I know you feel bad, but please try to remember."

"A day or two at the hospital? I don't like hospitals, Peter. They wake you up to give you sleeping pills, then wake you up again to see if the pills are working. They make you eat gruel and drink funny-colored things. I want my own bed."

I could hear myself whining, but I couldn't seem to stop myself. To add to my embarrassment, a tear rolled slowly down my cheek, leaving a crooked wet path that felt as though a garden snail had crawled down my face.

Joanie stopped sniffling and dried her cheeks with a tissue. "Don't be ridiculous, Claire. You've suffered a blow to the head, and it's imperative that you remain under constant medical supervision for forty-eight hours. The doctor said it was more than probable that you have a concussion, although it's impossible to determine how serious it may be. You are not leaving this room."

I tried to sit up, but my arms weren't cooperative and my back was downright rebellious. "Promise me no gruel," I said, trying to sound flippant, when I was more tempted to burst into a torrent of tears. "It's beginning to come back to me. . . . I attended the group meeting and talked to Candice, then went out to the sidewalk at about six o'clock. Maribeth came out of the fitness center and demanded to know what I'd been doing in the Ultima Center. I resorted to the truth, and she asked me if Gerald had been there. I admitted he hadn't been, which seemed to upset her. She drove away, stopped at the traffic light by the highway, and sat through a green light before turning around and coming back. Her driving was erratic enough to worry me—particularly when she seemed to be *aiming* for me. Candice came to the door of the Ultima Center and asked what was wrong. We went inside and were discussing what to do when . . . it became moot."

"Could you see Maribeth's face?" Peter asked. "Did she look normal?"

"I saw two headlights coming at me like something from a Stephen King novel," I replied acerbically. "I didn't trot around and tap on the car window."

Joanie sadly shook her head. "I think it's obvious that when Maribeth had driven the short distance, she realized she was having some sort of attack and headed back for assistance. By the time she reached the parking lot, she'd lost

all control and was helpless to avoid crashing into the front
of the Ultima Center. The whole thing is a tragic accident."

"Possibly," Peter murmured as he took out a small notebook and a pen. He frowned at me. "You said she was upset
because her husband was not at this meeting. Why would his
absence upset her?"

"It doesn't make sense," Joanie added, "in that Maribeth
said he was attending several meetings every week. Missing
one seems minor. Then again, she's been rather unpredictable this last week or so."

I wanted to pull the sheet over my face and make them
both disappear. Instead, I said, "There is only one officially
scheduled family support group each week, and it's the one
I sat through. Gerald may have told Maribeth he was going
to night sessions, but I think Maribeth had begun to realize
the truth. It was as obvious as the needle in my arm—and as
painful."

"As in private sessions with Candice?" Peter said, scrib-
bling in his notebook. "At the diet place, or at other, more
secluded places?"

"I don't know. Ask him."

Joanie put her hands on her hips and glowered down at
me. "You're not implying Maribeth went into a murderous
rage and drove into the Ultima Center with the express purpose of getting even with Candice, are you? You know her
better than that, Claire!"

I took a breath deep enough to make my back sting and
said, "No, I can't believe Maribeth did this on purpose,
although she's been noticeably weird lately. Both Candice
and Dr. Winder gave me some nonsense to explain away the
mood swings, but they have an interest in the Ultima program and the public perception of it as medically safe. You,
Peter, and I saw Maribeth lose her temper over insignificant
remarks. She also seemed spaced out on more than one occasion. Candice told me Gerald had been concerned to the
point that she recommended additional potassium caplets.
Furthermore, if Maribeth was experiencing a deficiency, she
might have made it worse with all the exercise."

Peter closed the notebook. "I'll have the hospital lab run a blood test to check on it. You try to get some rest, Claire; you're still in shock, whether you admit it or not." He gave me an avuncular kiss on the cheek and left the room.

Twisting her hands, Joanie paced around the room until she noticed my sagging eyelids, promised to visit later in the day, and tiptoed out the door. I drifted away to the relative tranquillity of Miss Wornewood's geography lesson.

After two days of tedium, I was allowed to exchange the pea-green environment for the decor of my own choosing (a dusty rose selected by a previous tenant). A sallow-faced volunteer rolled me in a wheelchair to a side door to make my escape. Peter was waiting by his car, and he'd brought several cushions and a blanket to protect my back, etc. The pain was enough to occupy me all the torturous miles to the apartment, up the hundreds of stairs, across the limitless prairie of the living room, and on to my bed.

Once I was settled, the pillow pleasingly plumped, the teacup conveniently placed, the blankets aesthetically aligned, I asked Peter if he'd confronted Gerald Galleston about his alleged affair with Candice Winder.

I was rewarded with an exasperated look. "Just this once," he said, turning on the long-suffering, what-have-I-done-to-deserve-this scowl, "I wish you'd stay out of this. I realize you know all the parties, but you had a severe blow to the head and only by a few inches missed having a piece of glass embedded in your heart. You need to turn off the curiosity and take it easy. No questions, no spate of deductive prowess, no anything. I'll go down to the bookstore and fetch you an armload of mystery novels. You can literally swim in the bed of intrigue."

"While you wait for Maribeth to wake up so that you can book her for homicide?"

"We're not booking anyone until we get some answers."

"Maybe you can rouse her with a cattle prod," I continued mercilessly. Hospital food can do that to you, especially that yellowish, lumpy stuff that congeals before you've finished toying with the canned peas.

"I'll suggest it to the attending physician. I need to go now, but I'll be by this evening with all the mysteries I can find in that musty place you so adore. Is there anything you need before I leave?"

"Would you plug Caron's telephone in here? No, don't leap to any unfounded conclusions; I simply don't feel up to getting out of bed for every siding salesman who's worried about my exterior peeling." I sank back and let out a brave little sigh. "My back feels as though someone has been playing tic-tac-toe on it with a branding iron, but if you're going to get upset, I'll manage somehow to climb out of bed every time the telephone rings."

He regarded me for a minute, unconvinced but also unsure, then went into Caron's room and returned with her telephone. He plugged it in, told me to call him at the station if I needed anything, spent another moment telling me how he'd have felt if the glass had entered my back a few inches higher, and let himself out the front door.

As soon as I heard the downstairs door close, I dialed the college switchboard and asked for Gerald's office number. I then dialed that number while gingerly wiggling around to find a position that didn't feel quite so much like lying on a bed of coals.

"Galleston here," he answered.

"This is Claire Malloy, Gerald. I hope I'm not disturbing you just before a class, but I wanted to convey my concern about Maribeth's condition."

"Ah, thank you, Claire."

"And poor Candice Winder," I added in the same melancholic tone. "Her husband must be devastated by her death." I listened to Gerald's unsteady breath for a minute, then took an unsteady one of my own and said, "Have you had the opportunity to speak to him about the . . . incident?"

"There have been a few conversations. Unpleasant ones, I'm afraid. He's very disturbed and has been making some wild accusations that have no basis in fact and come perilously close to slander. I'm most distressed. After all, my wife's in a coma and my car's in the shop, so I find myself reduced to hitchhiking rides with colleagues and coming home to an empty house. Maribeth is my primary concern, naturally, but the whole situation is intolerable. I haven't worked on my manuscript since the accident. Not one word.'' He paused for a moment, then cleared his throat. "You haven't been talking to Winder by any chance, have you?''

"I was released from the hospital this morning," I said, taking a small amount of pleasure from the undertone of strain in his voice. "I suppose I'll call him at some time to express my condolences. Have the funeral arrangements been announced?''

"I couldn't say. Listen, Claire, I need to talk to you, but I can't do it on my office telephone. There's no privacy here, but I could walk to your place after my eleven o'clock seminar is finished. In fact, I'll detour by Thurber Street and pick up sandwiches and a bottle of wine; we can have a cozy picnic on your bed. I'm sure you're much too sore in certain delicate areas to be up and about so soon. I do hope you'll allow me to do everything possible to ease the pain. Until noon, ma cherie?''

I agreed amiably, although the cozy picnic would not be conducted on my bed unless I died within the hour. During the subsequent sixty minutes, I gave death serious consideration as I eased on clothing, made it to the bathroom to comb my hair, made it to the kitchen to put on the teakettle and hide the wineglasses in the cupboard at the top of the back stairs, and finally found a moderately acceptable position on the sofa to await Gerald.

All of the above-mentioned activity had precluded thought. Now, gazing out the window at the treetops, I tried to find some explanation for the incident—or accident—or attempted murder (and then of whom—Candice or me?)—or whatever it was. With the exception of Maribeth, I knew almost nothing about those who might be involved. Dr. Winder was slick, professional, and no doubt armed with a bedside manner that might land him in bed with the more acquiescent clients. Each examination room was equipped with a padded paper-covered examination table; one rip and the evidence of misconduct was replaced with pristine white paper. Much easier than taking sheets to the Laundromat.

As for Bobbi Rodriquez, she seemed to be bobbing on a veritable sea of enthusiasm; if she was holding anything below the surface, it was not visible. I'd seen her going into Delano's Fitness Center and I'd seen her get into some hunk's car. I'd seen her newest leotard, for that matter.

The owner of Delano's Fitness Center was either genuinely enamored of Maribeth or genuinely enamored of being her inamorato when her impending fortune came due. Neither gave him any motive to wish her harm.

But Maribeth was the one who had harmed people—one terminally. She had mentioned that she wanted a divorce from Gerald, I recalled with a frown. Even if she had suddenly realized he was having an affair with Candice, she would hardly be inclined to risk her life—and mine—to come after Candice. Why would she care?

Because she was having a mental breakdown. Because she was lying when she declared she wanted a divorce. Because she wasn't after Candice but after me . . .

I ran out of theories just as I heard the downstairs bell ring. I hobbled to my door and yelled as loudly as I could for Gerald to come upstairs. He looked disappointed to find me fully clothed on the sofa, but produced a smile and held out a bottle of wine.

"A rosé, somewhat shy but with a lingering sweetness and a bouquet reminiscent of a spring shower," he said.

"I just look for the cork," I said dryly. "How's Maribeth? Has there been a change in her condition?"

He put the wine bottle on the coffee table and offered me a sandwich. When I shook my head, he sat beside me and ran his fingers through his hair. "No, I called the hospital before I left my office; she's exactly as she's been for the last two and a half days. They won't say a word about her prognosis. I'm increasingly worried that there might be permanent brain damage, that she'll remain in this coma indefinitely, simply vegetating, unaware of anyone or anything." His voice cracked and he turned his head to discreetly wipe his eyes. "Poor girl."

It would have been touching had I believed a syllable of it, but beneath his wretched tone I could hear the siding salesman offering me that once-in-a-lifetime opportunity to be the first kid on the block to be cloaked in aluminum.

"If she's that bad, you might as well divorce her," I said. "She wouldn't know the difference, would she?"

"But that would be treachery. I shall always be there for her, to manage her affairs and see that she is given the best treatment available." He picked up the wine bottle with a shaky hand. "Shall I fetch a corkscrew and two glasses? I do think you'll find this rosé quite a scintillating experience."

"I often find rosés to be, shall we say, unsubstantial. Tell me how you met Maribeth and fell in love."

"If I can remember," he muttered, not pleased with my dismissal of his shy yet sweet and showery wine selection. "Someone brought her to a party and then dumped her, I think. I took pity on her, chatted with her, and found myself obliged to drive her to her dormitory. We talked for a while about our respective childhoods and all that sort of drivel undergraduates consider 'sharing.' Eventually I discovered I'd grown fond of her. I suppose I imagined myself a modern-day Henry Higgins, willing to teach her how to behave in an intellectual environment, but she turned out to be less of an Eliza Doolittle than I'd hoped. Which is not to imply, of course, that I'm not truly worried about her now."

I could imagine Maribeth pouring out stories of her childhood in Farber Mansion to an attentive audience—right down to the amount of the trust fund coming to her on her thirtieth birthday. "She dropped out of school before she finished her degree, didn't she?"

"Yes, due to some problem from a childhood disease. They kept her in the school infirmary for months, and she missed too many classes to catch up. Where can I find a corkscrew? I'm terribly eager to try this little treasure, and I would be excited if you'd try a tiny sip. I picked it with you in mind, Claire. I find you shy, yet I suspect there's a sweet-ness just below the surface, a fragile yet deeply romantic desire to be swept into someone's arms and carried into the bedroom.''

"The corkscrew's on the counter and the sofa is just fine," I said flatly. When he returned with the corkscrew and two tumblers, I had moved all the way to the end of the sofa and curled my feet atop the middle cushion. He opened the wine and ceremoniously sniffed the cork before filling the glasses. I allowed him to take a mouthful of wine, then said, "I was surprised you haven't heard any information about Candice's funeral, but I guess it's awkward for the widower to call the lover."

He choked in a most satisfactory way. "The—*lover*? Whatever can you be talking about?"

"You didn't know? How quaint. It's the nonparticipatory spouse who's supposed to be the last to find out," I said, "but even Maribeth had it figured out. Three meetings a week? Really, Gerald, you might have at least read the sched-ule on the Ultima Center door. Wednesday, from five until six. We were short-changed last week, but I was not inclined to argue the point.''

"And you blabbed to the police," he said, his fingers tightening around the wineglass. "Some detective hinted as much, but I told him the truth: Candice and I may have had consultations in private, but only out of consideration for Maribeth's feelings. Had I attended those group meetings, I might have encountered someone I knew from the college, who would have told everyone on campus that she was so fat that she had to spend a fortune to go to the dieters' equivalent of Alcoholics Anonymous.''

"I see," I murmured. "And where did these consultations take place?"

He took a long sip of wine. "Is this any of your business, my dearest Claire? I thought you were worried about Mari-beth, not about a bunch of boring consultations at the Ultima Center."

"I'm always being accused of meddling. Now, what did you want to talk to me about, Gerald?"

"Another matter entirely," he said as he polished off the wine and refilled his glass. "Are you sure you won't join me? What I needed to ask you is if you're willing to testify to Maribeth's inexplicable behavior the last few days before the accident? There may be some question of liability for the damage to the building and the . . . the unfortunate demise of one of the owners. I think it prudent to confirm that she was incapable of rational thought or action, which would serve to reinforce my contention that she was not responsible for the damages resulting from the crash. Once we've established that, the insurance company will be obligated to settle any claims."

"How do you account for it?" I asked curiously.

"Beats me." He drank the contents of my glass, refilled his own again, and gave me a seductive smile. "I mentioned it to Candice, and she said it might be something to do with the potassium or protein. Something like that. Jesus H., after all I've been through lately, how am I supposed to remember that? Whatever it was, Candice gave me a bottle of pills to take to Maribeth, which I did." His seductive, if somewhat blurred, smile disappeared as his eyes narrowed. "Do you think the pills were poison? I sure as hell won't have any problems with liability if Candice poisoned Maribeth. I'd be home free and clear, I would!"

The above speech was not given nearly as clearly as indicated by the crisp print of prose. Gerald was rapidly getting bombed; his sandwich was untouched but the bottle of rosé was almost empty. He was attempting to look crafty, but a certain lack of focus destroyed the effect, and he was having difficulty coaxing the wine into the glass.

"Why would Candice want to poison Maribeth?" I prodded, as willing as anyone to take advantage of a drunk.

"I dunno. How about one teeny tiny sip of rosé, honey? It's shy and sweet and very, very nice."

I shook my head politely. "I thought Candice was very,

very nice, too. She had such a warm smile and a real concern for her clients."

"Big knockers. She had the biggest damn knockers I've seen in all my days, and I've seen some damn big ones." He ogled at mine, then made a face and said, "They were a lot bigger than yours. That's for sure. You ever thought about silicone injections?"

"I'll think about it tonight. My goodness, look at the time. You're going to have to hurry if you don't want to miss your class, Gerald. I strongly suggest you take the sandwiches with you and eat them while you walk back to your office."

"Don't have a class for another hour." He tipped the glass back so far that wine splattered on his nose, then banged it down and drank the remaining wine from the bottle with noisy gulps. "We got all the time in the world, Claire. We can do all kinda stuff. Hey, you're not mad about what I said, are you? Your knockers are plenty big enough for me. I'm more of a leg man anyway."

He lunged just as I turned my leg and lifted my knee, and his midriff slammed down against it. Air whooshed out of his lungs. He gave me a wounded look, then his eyes rolled upward and he sprawled across my lap. The unexpected pressure made me feel as if I were sitting in a pool of lava.

"Get off me," I growled, shaking his shoulder as I fought back tears. "Come on, Gerald, I'm sure you've got a faculty meeting, or a long-distance telephone call."

He mumbled and began to burrow toward my crotch.

"Stop this," I said, now shaking his shoulder hard enough to frappe his brain. "Stop this right now, damn it!"

To make things more exciting, I heard a knock at the door. I shook Gerald furiously as I imagined Peter's face when he opened the door. Poor Claire, bedridden and too weak to walk to the telephone, with a suspect's husband attempting to gnaw through her zipper while too drunk to uncross his eyes. The knock was repeated.

Gerald had managed to worm his arm around me, and for all intents and purposes, was glued to my thighs. No explanations came to mind. Exerting as much pull as I could on his arm, I yelled, "Go away! I'm too sore to come to the door."

Joanie opened the door and said, "I heard you coming home earlier, and I brought you some soup for lunch. Shall I warm it up in the kitchen?"

From the doorway the back of the sofa must have blocked her view of the problem, but as she started for the kitchen she saw it. Or the back of its head, to be precise. "What in heaven's name. . . ?" she gasped, her pace faltering.

"Would you help me roll him off, please? He's remarkably heavy at the moment, and uncooperative."

"Why, that's Gerald . . ." she continued. "I'm afraid I don't understand what it is the two of you are doing."

"Stop worrying about it and drag him off of me," I said through clenched teeth. "He's drunker than a barroom brawler, and equally beyond reason. If you don't do something soon, my gynecologist is in for a shock. Don't just stand there—*help me.*"

It took both of us to drag him off of me, and I enjoyed the resounding thud of his body hitting the floor. It seemed to jar some sense back in him, and after a few false starts, he unsteadily made it to his feet.

"Good day, ladies. Please excuse me," he said with the teetering dignity of a drunk, then turned around and went out the door.

I held my breath until I heard the downstairs door close. "It's a bit tricky to explain," I said to Joanie, who was still staring at me. "He had something he wanted to discuss with me, but he was distracted by a bottle of wine on an empty stomach and ended up thoroughly drunk."

"In your lap."

"He's a leg man," I said weakly. "Have you heard anything about Maribeth's condition?"

She sat down across from me, placed the pan of soup on the floor, and leaned forward. "Her condition hasn't changed, but I did learn something from my friend Betty Lou Kirkpatrick, who does volunteer work at the hospital a few hours every week. She prefers the gift shop, but yesterday they were understaffed on several of the wards and asked the volunteers to run errands for the nurses, wheel patients to X-ray and back, that sort of thing. I met Betty Lou last year at a Fighting Frog basketball game. She's an absolutely charming woman. Her daughter teaches here at the law school, and one of her four sons is a doctor in Scotland, another an attorney, a third is in California—''

''Would you please get to the point? I've had a rough day thus far, and certain areas of my anatomy are screaming.''

''Drinking wine with another woman's husband can be tiring,'' Joanie said with a sniff. ''Out of consideration for your anatomy, I shall continue. Betty Lou was in the intensive care ward, waiting to escort a patient to a private room, when she heard a conversation from the next cubicle. She is by no means nosy, but she did rear five children and learned early in the game the importance of listening to all conversations conducted in whispers. One of the whisperers was referred to as Lieutenant Rosen, the other as Dr. Horne or Haynes or something like that. She said the two were discussing a patient's urinalysis results.''

''And—what?'' I said. ''What did Betty Lou hear?''

Joanie leaned back and crossed her legs, gave me a smug smile, and said, ''She heard the doctor telling the lieutenant that the Galleston girl had a severe potassium deficiency, so severe that he was surprised she could walk around the week before the accident, in that her mental acuity would be that of a stalk of asparagus. Betty Lou said she thought that was a vulgar remark, especially from a professional who—''

''What else did she hear?''

''That's it. They moved away from the curtain, and the orderlies finished settling the patient in the wheelchair. Betty Lou said she had no choice but to wheel the old man away.''

I flopped back on the sofa, realized I'd made a serious error, and rolled over onto my stomach. ''But Maribeth said that Gerald had brought her a bottle of potassium caplets, and he said the same thing before he turned ugly a little while ago. If she'd been taking the caplets all along, and then began taking extra doses, why would she have this severe deficiency?''

"I have no idea," Joanie said, glancing at her watch. "I've got a class in fifteen minutes. I'll put the soup on the stove, but you'll have to serve yourself when it's ready. We're throwing today, so I need to change."

"Throwing up? Throwing fits? Throwing the baby out with the bathwater?''

"Throwing pots. I'll come up for the pan after the funeral," she said as she carried the soup into the kitchen, clicked a knob, and headed for the front door.

"The funeral?" I repeated.

"Candice Winder's funeral, today at four o'clock. It's at that funeral home near the bypass, in their chapel. I'm not sure whether it's to be followed by interment or cremation."

I listened to her footsteps as she went down to her apartment. Candice's funeral was in three hours. I decided that if I started immediately, or after a bowl of soup, then I could be dressed in funerary finery and ready to go with a good five minutes to spare.

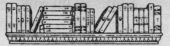

EIGHT

I had just discovered, amazingly enough, that one agitates muscles not only in one's back but also in one's buttocks in the process of combing one's hair, when Caron and Inez tumbled into the bathroom with their typical lack of reserve.

"Are you okay?" Caron demanded, although we'd discussed the issue numerous times during my incarceration. "You look all pale and, well, sort of frowsy."

"Your hair," Inez elaborated in an awed whisper.

"It seems that when you raise your arms, certain muscles are stretched upward. The muscles are sore, and thus the arms are not enthusiastic to do their duty."

Caron and Inez studied the areas in question, looking as though they were fighting back snickers. I gazed at myself in the mirror and concluded that "frowsy" was a compliment. Discarding the comb, I said, "How's the popcorn and grapefruit juice diet coming? Lost any weight?"

Caron picked up my comb and ran it through her hair. "It was going just fine, but then Rhonda talked to her cousin and found out we weren't supposed to butter and salt the popcorn. Have you ever tried to choke down dry, unsalted popcorn? It's worse than eating pieces of Styrofoam. We nearly gagged, didn't we, Inez?''

"It was yucky," Inez said loyally, "although I'm not sure what Styrofoam tastes like."

"So what diet are you on now?" I asked.

"A vastly superior one," Caron said. "We bought this box of diet-aid candy at the drugstore. We have two or three pieces before each meal, along with a glass of warm water, and they sort of expand and kill your appetite."

"Is it working?"

Caron nudged me aside to take full possession of the mirror. "Not yet, but the candy's pretty good. How come you're dressed like that? I thought you were supposed to stay in bed for a few more days, in case you're going to turn into a werewolf or something."

"I have to attend a funeral," I said, sighing as I considered the drive to the funeral home. "Would you like to drive me there?"

Caron had whined and pouted herself into a learner's permit several months ago. Peter had given her a few lessons; I myself had refused to entertain such folly, but now I realized it might be better to pad the passenger's side with pillows or lounge face down in the back seat.

"Do we have to go to the funeral?" she said, clearly gripped with a heady dose of approach-avoidance. "I don't like funerals, you know. All those people sniveling and snuffling, and the sickly smell of the flowers, not to mention the casket. I mean, it's a real downer. I could drive you to the mall, or to a pizza place, or even around town." She gave me an appraising smile. "You need some fresh air, Mother. We can drive out toward one of the little towns, then—"

"The funeral home or nowhere at all."

"How about if we drop you off and then come back later?"

"You're not allowed to drive anywhere without a licensed adult in the car," I said firmly. "Take books or the box of candy, and you can wait in the car during the service."

Inez gulped nervously. "My grandmother's funeral lasted more than an hour, and then we had to hang around while all these people shook our hands and went on and on about Granny and her parakeets. She had fifty-four of them.''

"Why?" Caron said.

"She was allergic to cats."

"I'm allergic to shellfish, but that doesn't mean I collect boa constrictors."

Inez blinked. "That's different—you hate snakes. Granny loved her little parakeets."

"It's up to you," I inserted. "I'm going to get my purse, some pillows, and the car key. If you don't want to risk a long wait outside, then I'll see if I can catch Joanie. She didn't say that she was coming back to change, but she might, and she may be willing to drive me."

I left the two debating the pet poser, got my things together, and stood by the front door. Eventually Caron stalked out of the bathroom with Inez in tow and held out her hand for the key.

"We'll wait," she said coolly, "but they'd better not get too carried away with this funeral service. The person's dead, for pity's sake. There's no point in going On And On about it; the star of the show can't hear it.''

Once in the garage, I decided it was wiser for me to cower in the backseat of my battered hatchback, where I would be less inclined to offer editorials. Peter had said she was doing fairly well; then again, he'd made quite a few misevaluations of my invaluable assistance during official investigations. I arranged my pillows, buckled my seat belt as tightly as I could bear, gave her precise directions, closed my eyes, and bleakly told her to have at it.

After a series of false starts, the car hiccupped out of the garage, died in the driveway, was coaxed to life, and sputtered its way to the edge of the street. I clamped my teeth on my lower lip and tried to think of balmy spring afternoons, quiet evenings with a good novel, serene sessions in the bubbly, more active sessions with the cop. And could think of nothing but the nightmarish scene when Maribeth seemed to be determined to run me down in the Ultima parking lot.

Maribeth of the severe potassium deficiency, so severe the

doctor had compared her mental capacity to that of a stalk of asparagus. No wonder she had experienced such difficulty driving; perhaps, as Joanie said, she had returned to the parking lot for help, then lost control and crashed into the front of the store. All that made some sense, although I couldn't figure out why she'd developed the deficiency in the first place.

A car's horn blared, jarring me out of my thoughts. I peered over the edge of the front seat. "We seem to be straddling the middle line," I said evenly.

"I know," Caron growled, her fingers white around the steering wheel, nicely contrasting with her scarlet neck. "But that's no reason for everybody to get nasty. You'd think no one ever had to scoot over just a tiny bit." She rolled down the window, and shouted, "Whatsa matter, buddy? Spill a cup of ice in your lap?"

"Caron!" I said. "Is this what Peter taught you to do? If you don't roll up the window this second, I'll—I'll put both of you on the sidewalk, lock the car, and call a taxi."

"Yeah, yeah, but he didn't have any reason to make that gesture at me," she muttered as she stepped on the accelerator. The car took off like a sprinter, fast enough to fling me backward and knock any further remarks out of my mouth.

There were more honks and presumably more gestures, but I gritted my teeth, kept my eyes closed, and somehow we made it to the funeral home without injury. Once the engine died, I sat up in time to see Bobbi Rodriquez and Jody Delano going through the front door. Bobbi wore a dark dress, the hemline of which came down at least halfway to her knees. Jody wore a more conventional suit and tie, although he tugged at his collar as if he wished he were wearing a well-ripened, redolent sweatshirt.

"Who was that?" Caron said abruptly.

"The girl that works—or worked—at the Ultima Center. She's into leotards and sweat." I found my purse, which had fallen to the floor during one of the more enthusiastic hiccups, and began to edge toward the car door, keenly aware of every splinter of glass that had pierced my epidermis.

"The *guy*, Mother. Who was the guy?"

"He owns a fitness center. This shouldn't take too long, and I expect you to sit right here and not pull any tricks. Understand?"

"Gee," Caron said in a superficially sympathetic voice, "there aren't very many people going to the funeral. That's kind of sad, isn't it?"

She must have jabbed Inez, because the latter let out a muffled grunt and said, "The family's going to feel bad if no one comes to show respect for the deceased."

"I'm impressed with your compassion," I said as I opened the door and began the arduous ascent to my feet. Sir Edmund probably had a less painful trip to the top of Everest. "All this worry about the family's feelings indicates a great deal of maturity—and all developed in the last twenty minutes, too. How utterly astounding."

"Oh, Mother," Caron said, "you always underestimate me. Besides, you look like you're going to fall on your face any minute. Inez and I had better help you inside before you do something Too Humiliating for Words."

My little saints got out of the car and solicitously took my arms. Feeling no more senile than any permanent resident of a nursing home, I allowed them to escort me into the foyer, where we encountered a elderly man in a sober suit and a suitably sober expression.

"Yes?" he inquired. "Are you here for the service, or" —he ran a professional eye over me—"to make some kind of arrangement for the future, when we can be of assistance to your loved ones in their time of grief and mourning?"

"I told you to put on makeup," Caron whispered fiercely in my ear. "He thinks you're a walking cadaver."

"We're here for the service for Candice Winder," I said.

"Of course you are," he said with a faintly incredulous smile. "The service is in the Remembrance Chapel, to the left. If you'll spend a moment looking it over, I think you'll find it small yet surprisingly comfortable, able to accommodate more than fifty mourners. With the judicious placement of folding chairs, we've been able to squeeze in as many as seventy-five. I personally chose the decor and insisted on a state-of-the-art quadrophonic sound system. We have more than two hundred musical selections, ranging from the traditional to the more lively contemporary works. If you're interested, after the service I'll be happy to take you on a tour of the rest of our facilities. We're a full-service mortuary, which can drastically reduce the cost of a first-class funeral.''

I vowed never to die as long as I lived, curled a lip at the ghoul, and took off for the chapel door, dragging Caron and Inez with me. There would be no need of judiciously placed folding chairs. Sheldon Winder sat in the first pew, his head cradled in his hands. Three pews behind him sat Bobbi and Jody, their shoulders touching and their heads together as they talked softly. About a dozen others, obviously Ultima clients, were scattered throughout the pews, some dabbing their eyes with tissues and others obediently assessing the decor and awaiting quadrophonic music.

I spotted a familiar head of hair and slipped in beside Joanie Powell, who was neither dabbing nor assessing but merely sitting with her hands folded in her lap. She gave me a wan smile, then noticed Caron and Inez.

"What are they doing here?" she said tartly. "For that matter, what are you doing here? Aren't you under orders to stay in bed?"

Before I could answer, Gerald Galleston slunk down a side aisle and sat down in the pew directly opposite Bobbi and Jody. He mopped his forehead with a handkerchief, then settled back and shot a dark look at the back of Sheldon's head.

Caron and Inez were buzzing at each other, so I hissed at them to be quiet and turned back to Joanie. "The doctor had no objection," I lied, "and I felt like I ought to come, especially since I was there when it happened. Had Candice and I been standing the other way around, I'd be tucked away in a satin-lined casket, and . . ." I gestured vaguely toward the front of the room. "Where is the casket?"

"This is a memorial service. She's already been cremated," Joanie explained.

Caron poked me in the side. "Guess who's here, Mother."

I slowly swiveled my head until I caught sight of a glowering face in the back pew, then turned back and sighed. Joanie might have fallen for my slight misrepresentation of the doctor's orders, but Peter had been in the hospital cell when I had agreed meekly not to set foot out of bed for an additional forty-eight hours. I had my fingers crossed at the time, naturally, but I had a feeling that Peter wouldn't be pleased with my minor junket. Wondering if I could blame it on a concussion, I shrank down in the pew.

A minister in his early thirties came out a side door as music flowed through unseen speakers. He folded his hands and rocked on his feet through the first selection—blessedly of the more traditional bent—suggested we pray, admitted he'd never met Candice Angelica Carruthers Winder but had been assured by her family and friends that she was a warm, loving person whom we would all remember as such, and in general conducted a generic service.

Once the final notes had faded, the minister shook Sheldon's hand and disappeared through the side door. The Ultima clients stood up and began to squeeze themselves out of the pews. Joanie was stirring, but I had no intention of moving from my position, in that I knew what (who) awaited me at the door. I was not overcome with anticipation.

Sheldon rose, stopped briefly to straighten the creases in his trousers, then turned and saw Bobbi and Jody. "What are you doing here, Delano?"

Jody scratched his head. "Sitting here like everybody else, I guess."

"It can't be as amusing as engaging in unnatural sex in the Jacuzzi."

"Oh, Shelly," Bobbi said, "don't be like that. Jody and I just wanted to pay our respects. I mean, like, I worked with Candice for five weeks, and she was so super and my very best friend. We had lunch together and everything."

Sheldon smirked. "How about you, Galleston? That minister was correct when he talked about all of Candice's dear friends—some dearer than others."

I wasn't sure what all this meant, but I was entranced, as

was Joanie on one side, Caron and Inez on the other, and the various clients in their various stages of disengagement. No doubt the cop in the last row was taking it in, too.

"Now see here," Gerald said pompously, "I'm willing to make allowances because of the situation, but I won't stand for slanderous remarks made in public about my relationship with Candice. She was counseling me on how best to support Maribeth during the diet. If you want to make that into an international incident, be prepared to find yourself slapped with a lawsuit."

"Some of those counseling sessions lasted until midnight, didn't they?" Winder continued unpleasantly. "Were you discussing how best to support Maribeth—or how best to keep her so addled she wouldn't resist commitment to a psycho ward? Did you have the papers neatly drawn up?"

"She was addled because of your damn diet, Winder. Now she's in a coma, and you may find yourself explaining the details of the program to a jury."

"Oh, Shelly," Bobbi said. She looked at the floor and shook her head.

One of the clients, a middle-aged woman with a weathered face and spiky hair, popped loose from the pew and marched down the aisle. "Sorry about the accident, Dr. Winder," she said gruffly, holding out her hand. "Candice was a nice woman and a fine nurse. I wouldn't have lost thirty-seven pounds without her support."

"Ms. Koenig, how very kind," he mumbled. After a moment, he was surrounded by the clients, each competing with the others to claim Candice was responsible for his or her weight loss. Numbers were being flung out rather loudly, considering our locale, and Sheldon was looking increasingly panicked by the unruly mob. Gerald, Jody, and Bobbi availed themselves of the golden opportunity to leave without further conversation with the chief mourner.

Caron nudged me and said, "Isn't he kind of young to be an aerobics teacher?"

I could see all kinds of insidious things floating behind her guileless eyes. "He's not as young as he looks. Furthermore, he enjoys making his victims sweat like iced tea glasses on a hot day. He revels in it. He shouts things about kicking higher and doing sit-ups faster and getting your knees up to your chin. Then, when you think you're home free, he sends you into the innermost circles of inferno to be boiled and baked.''

"How old is he?'' Caron said, twisting her head to catch a last glimpse of the sadist. "He can't be that old.''

"He's old enough to escort a college girl to a funeral.'' I did not mention he also was old enough to pursue a twenty-nine-year-old married woman. I grabbed the back of the pew to pull myself up. "I'm going to offer my condolences to Dr. Winder,'' I added with a wince. "Why don't you and Inez wait in the car?''

The two scurried away, no doubt hoping to catch another glimpse of Jody in the parking lot. Joanie said she'd stop by in the evening with a casserole, then followed the girls out of the chapel. I was aware Peter was still glued to his pew, but I refused to acknowledge it and made my way down front, where Sheldon had beaten off all but a couple of the Ultima clients.

As I approached they drifted away, and he gave me a bland smile. "I'm glad to see you've recovered from the dreadful accident, Ms. Malloy. It was unfortunate that you were present when it occurred, but fortunate that you had your back turned.''

"Fortunate,'' I murmured. "I regret Candice and I hadn't gone into the office, where we'd have been somewhat protected from the glass, but we were by the door, trying to decide what to do. Maribeth's behavior was''—I gave him an equally bland smile—"so odd that we were alarmed. Today I heard a rumor that she had a severe potassium deficiency.''

"Impossible. After you mentioned it to me, I looked over her file. According to Candice's notation, Maribeth was taking the standard three hundred milligrams daily; she was given a seven-day supply every Monday. The day before the accident she was instructed to take an additional one hundred fifty milligrams daily, just to be safe. I believe Candice sent the bottle home with Maribeth's husband.''

"Could the potassium caplets have been so old they'd lost their potency?" I asked.

"Absolutely not. They were ordered less than three months ago from a reputable pharmaceutical company. I've got the invoices to prove it, and I don't appreciate this insinuation that Ultima Diet Center would give its clients anything but the newest and best dietary supplements.''

I moved closer, hoping it might induce him to lower his voice. "Where are they stored? Are they kept in a locked cupboard?"

"Ms. Malloy," he said, aggrieved and not one decibel quieter, "vitamins and supplements do not fall into the same category as controlled substances such as codeine and morphine. Diet centers are not plagued by junkies in search of a fix; there is no black market for calcium. We keep our supplies in a cabinet in the office, so they can be dispensed with a minimum of delay.''

"Then someone could have tampered with the potassium?"

"Ms. Malloy," he said again, almost shouting now, "your veiled accusations are untenable. The only people with access to the office were Candice, Bobbi, and myself; we did not run off spare keys and distribute them on street corners. And why would someone desire to tamper with a bottle of potassium caplets? As a practical joke? As a way to cause a driving accident? What are you intimating, Ms. Malloy?"

The sensation in my back was very much as if a sliver of glass was imbedded there, and I knew whence it came. I wiped my face, his tirade having been moist, and said in a very low voice, "I wasn't intimating anything, Dr. Winder; I was just trying to understand how Maribeth could have had a potassium deficiency so severe she lost control of her car. You prescribed the dosage, Candice delivered it, and somehow Maribeth ended up without it.''

"Then she failed to follow instructions. We at Ultima can offer supervision and support, but we can't follow our clients home to make sure they're adhering religiously to the program. We have plenty of clients who claim they've put not one illegal bite in their mouths, then find themselves admitting to a hot fudge sundae—with extra whipped cream—when faced with the scales.''

"But Maribeth told me she was taking the potassium.''

He gave me a condescending look. "People lie, Ms. Malloy. Surely you're old enough to have learned that. If you'll excuse me, I must settle up with the funeral director. Should you ever put on unwanted weight, please don't hesitate to call us. At Ultima, if you don't lose, we don't win.'' He brushed past me and went up the aisle and out the door.

Peter had made himself comfortable in the pew, his legs crossed and one arm draped across the back. His notebook lay beside him. As I attempted to sail by, he flashed all two hundred white teeth and said, "Do you have time for coffee before you go home? You look a little haggard.''

"I'd love to," I said, my fingers crossed tightly behind my back, "but Caron and Inez are waiting for me in the car. Caron drove me over, and I'll have to ride back with her, not matter how appalling the idea. Are you sure she's learned anything from your driving lessons?''

He rose like a lanky old cowhand, all teeth and twinkly eyes and amiability. "Sergeant's Jorgeson's waiting outside. He can accompany the girls and explain some of the finer points of successful demolition driving. That way we can have ourselves a nice quiet conversation.''

I would have preferred to eat gravel. "That's not a very nice thing to do to Jorgeson," I said as we left the chapel. "He may have better things to do than flirt with death.''

"But I shall explain how much I'm looking forward to being alone with you," Peter said silkily, then went over to his car and bent down to talk to Jorgeson.

I went to the driver's side of my car and tapped on the window to gain Caron's attention. She rolled down the window. "One of Peter's men is going to ride home with you," I said. "If you yell at anyone, he'll ticket you for public obscenity. In that no one will come forward to post bail, you may find yourself wasting away in jail. On the other hand, they may serve starchy food for budgetary reasons, and you'll be a blimp before you're paroled.''

"You are so amusing, Mother." She glanced at Inez. "This diet-aid candy hasn't worked thus far, and we're probably going to give it up. What we really need to do is just stick to a sensible diet and get lots of exercise. That way when we lose all the weight, our skin won't hang in gross, flabby flaps that tremble when we walk.''

"Jogging? Swimming laps at the youth center? How about the videocassette you watched so diligently from the sofa?''

"Maybe," she said, feigning consideration of my bright suggestions. "We were thinking we might join a regular aerobics class so we'd have to work out two or three times a week.''

"Try the one at the youth center," I said. I stepped back as a very leery Jorgeson got in the backseat and began issuing orders. Once he'd gotten them out of the parking lot, I reluctantly went to Peter's car and eased my weary fanny into the passenger's seat.

He reached into the back and wordlessly handed me a pillow. I wiggled around as best I could, sighing like a leaky tire in hopes of eliciting sympathy. "I've always heard that time flies," he said, "but your forty-eight hours in bed must have created a sonic boom or two. I left you at about eleven this morning and saw you here at four o'clock. I'm just a plodding cop, but even I can do the arithmetic on this one.''

"Oh, shut up," I said without rancor. "I felt as if I had to come to the funeral. The only headache I've had is the one you're giving me right now. No, that's not true—the ride over here with Caron wasn't exactly soporific. Besides, you wrote off the death as an accident caused by Maribeth's potassium deficiency, so shouldn't you be at the football field looking for steroid pushers or searching lockers or ordering athletes to pee in little bottles?''

"Are you trying to change the subject?''

"Damn straight. Are the feds still lurking under the bleachers?''

He continued to look forward, but a nerve twitched on his rigidly set jaw and his expression was that of a televangelist preparing to let 'er rip. "And how did you hear of that?" he said in a surprisingly normal voice for a person with lockjaw.

"I read about it in the newspaper."

"Oh." He drove into the parking lot of the bowling alley and cut off the engine, then came around the car and opened the door for me, all the while giving me an unfathomable look. I'd seen it before, and although I hadn't fathomed it, I knew it did not bode well. We went into the restaurant and found an unoccupied booth. The Formica table was grimy, and the booth padded with red plastic held down by strips of silver tape. The other patrons eyed as coldly, as if we'd invaded a private sanctuary, before resuming their conversations, presumably of bowling balls and such.

A tired waitress with bleached hair and a discouraged expression dropped two menus on the table and promised to come back at some point in the future.

"So what did you learn from reading the newspaper so thoroughly?" Peter asked in a soft voice reinforced with steel rods.

I glanced over my shoulder. "What are we doing in this place?" I whispered.

"We're having coffee. Again, what did you learn?"

"Not to let you pick the next restaurant. I merely read what was in the paper, which wasn't very much. A football player had a heart attack caused by steroids in his system. Steroids are not only dangerous, they're illegal. The college officials are embarrassed, and the NAACP is investigating, although I don't know why unless the player was black." I gave him a charmingly bewildered shrug. "Smollenski sounds like an Eastern European name."

"The NAACP is not investigating; the NCAA, as in National Collegiate Athletics Association, is conducting the investigation. If they find any evidence that the player was supplied with steroids by anyone involved in the athletics department, they'll bring sanctions against the college."

"And you'll file charges, I hope. How dreadful to think a coach or a trainer would give players dangerous drugs. The primary reason these boys are enrolled in college is to get an education, not to kill themselves for the team."

Peter seemed to find this outburst humorous and was still chuckling when the waitress returned with two glasses of water and a pad. "What'll it be?" she droned. "Special's chicken-fried steak and mashed potatoes, choice of vegetable. Drink's included; dessert's extra. Lemon icebox pie, carrot cake, or vanilla ice cream."

I eyed the lipstick smudge on the glass in front of me and declined to order anything. Peter ordered coffee, managed to stop chuckling, and reached across the table to put his hand on mine. "Listen to me, please. We've got our eye on one of the backfield coaches, an ambitious young guy who'd like to spawn enough all-star players to earn a promotion. One of his protégés has indicated a willingness to talk; we'll be able to ask for a warrant in the next few days—if the player doesn't panic and leave town."

"So it's very hush-hush," I said in a dramatic whisper. "I shouldn't say a word to any of the football players when I have them over for tea tomorrow, right? I'll be as quiet as a spy who stays out in the cold." I waited while the waitress banged down a chipped cup on a cracked saucer. "If you're still trying to nail this coach, shouldn't you be closeted with the national whatever people and the feds? And if you've closed the investigation of Maribeth's accident, what were you doing at Candice's funeral?"

"Who said we'd closed that investigation?"

"Haven't you written it off as caused by a potassium deficiency?"

"Where'd you hear that?"

"I hear things," I said modestly. "I think you're wrong, of course, because you heard Maribeth say she would be more careful not to miss the prescribed caplets. Then again, I suppose you had the lab run a test on the caplets to make sure they were what they were purported to be, so you may be right after all. It's rather difficult to give Gerald a motive; he's very interested in Maribeth's continued well-being until the trust comes to her on her birthday." Peter was beginning to make rabid-dog noises, so I took a breath and continued. "But if Gerald and Candice were having an affair, then Candice might wish Maribeth was out of the picture, so she could marry Gerald. She certainly had access to the potassium caplets; maybe she substituted them with a placebo of some kind. But that might not play, if you've already gotten the lab report." I gave him a bright, inquisitive look, although somewhere in my soul I knew I was teetering on a threadbare tightrope in the very top of the tent.

Peter sipped his coffee, wrinkled his nose, and carefully put down the cup, all the while gazing at me through impenetrable eyes. He curled a finger at the waitress, who with Houdini-ish insight came to the table and slapped down the check, then went to the adjoining booth to drone about the specials. He looked at the check, took a dollar from his billfold and tucked it under the cracked saucer, and stood up. "Shall we go?"

"I was only asking," I muttered as we went out to the car. "If you didn't have the potassium tested, say so, and I'll drop the matter."

His teeth reminded me of blunted icicles as he smiled, and his voice was of arctic origin. "You'll drop the matter, you say?" He held the car door open for me, waited for me to snuggle on top of the pillow, then closed the door and went around the car and took his place behind the wheel. "I don't want to cast doubts on your basic honesty, but you've said that before, and it hasn't even played in Boston, much less Cleveland. I realize you're not going to tell me the source of your information, and we broke the last set of thumbscrews last week"—he was silent until he'd turned the car around and started for the street—"but you might consider the sensation of seventeen splinters of glass in your backside." He jerked the wheel so that we bounced over a pothole, then glanced at me as I let out a muffled groan. "Meddling can be painful." He found an asphalt speed breaker and did not brake. "Disobeying the doctor's orders can be unwise."

As he aimed for yet another speed breaker, I said, "Will you please stop this, Peter? I am not a child to be punished for disobedience. I am an adult—at the moment a very angry adult. If you hit that bump, I will get out of this car and hitchhike home."

He eased off the gas pedal and turned the car back toward the street. "I was trying to make a point, Claire. I can't count the number of times you've had a gun aimed at you, and by a person who had nothing to lose by pulling the trigger. I don't want to lose you."

"Not that many times." I sniffed, my fanny stinging as sharply as my pride. "When I deduced the identity of Azalea Twilight's murderer, perhaps, and in the lobby of the Mimosa Inn during the mock-murder weekend, and that one time at the theater. I'm surprised you can't count to three, Lieutenant Rosen; have some of your fingers fallen off when you weren't looking?" Armed with bravado, I'll say most anything.

"Not bad for a mild-mannered bookseller," he said as we left the parking lot. "A mild-mannered civilian bookseller who needs to mind her own business rather than meddling in official investigations."

"Don't you ever tire of saying that? In any case, there is no official investigation of Maribeth's so-called mishap, so there's no way I can meddle in one, is there? And I promise to stay out of the locker room, so you can't claim I'm meddling in that one."

As we stopped at a red light, I noticed my car in the next lane. The driver was exceedingly grim. The front-seat passenger was stoic but blinking several times a second. The backseat appeared to be empty.

"Where's Jorgeson?" I gasped.

Peter stared at the car. Before he could say anything, a hand appeared from the depths of the backseat and a finger limply waggled. Caron's lower lip shot out, and the car squealed away from the light, which, to someone's mother's heartfelt relief, had turned green.

As had someone's mother.

NINE

"The police refuse to investigate?" Joanie Powell said, her fork poised halfway to her mouth. "Maribeth had a potassium deficiency, but no one's mind is inquiring enough to wonder how it happened?" She propelled the fork the remaining inches and chomped angrily.

"That's about it," I admitted. I was in my bathrobe and on my sofa, both of which had done wonders to soothe fanny and pride. Joanie's casserole was helping, too, along with Caron and Inez's absence, in that they'd grudgingly gone to the youth center near the high school to find out about inexpensive aerobics classes. I could hardly wait to hear their opinions, and I was sure I would—at great length.

"Then what are we going to do?" Joanie asked. "We can't sit around while Maribeth remains in a coma caused by someone who's now convinced he or she got away with it."

Sighing, I said, "Peter never answered my question, but I think we can assume they didn't run any tests on Maribeth's potassium supply. According to Sheldon Winder, the supplements were kept in an unlocked cabinet in the Ultima office, but he, Candice, and Bobbi had the only keys to the center. It's possible all three of them could have been with clients in the examinations rooms at the same time, leaving the office vacant, but it'd be risky for anyone to sneak in for even a few seconds. If for no other reason, a client might come in the front door and accuse you of peeking at her confidential folder.''

"I certainly wouldn't want my weight to appear in the campus newspaper gossip column.''

"They contain medical information, too.'' I rose and went to the kitchen, moving slowly not only out of consideration for my much abused body but also because something was nagging at me and I couldn't quite grab it. Medical information, I reiterated mentally. The Ultima Center took medical histories and ran tests before enrolling its clients. But had they run tests on Maribeth? I poured myself a medicinal shot of scotch and went back into the living room, scowling like a copy editor confronted with capricious punctuation.

Once I was resettled, I said, "When I asked Gerald why Maribeth dropped out of college, he was vague, saying only that she'd stayed in the infirmary for several months and missed too many classes. Do you know what was wrong with her?''

Joanie thought for a moment, then shook her head. "No, and since it happened while Maribeth was in college, I doubt my daughter would know, either; they'd quit corresponding by then. I guess I could ask her when she calls tonight. Do you think it's important?''

"I have no idea,'' I said morosely. "Maybe Maribeth had some bizarre illness that subsequently prevented her body from absorbing potassium. Maybe she had something wrong with her throat and could no longer swallow caplets. Maybe I'm making no sense whatsoever.'' In that I was holding a glass, I resisted the urge to throw up my hands in the traditional gesture of defeat and instead drank a good inch of scotch.

"I'll ask my daughter tonight, and I'll also call Betty Lou and find out when she's on duty at the hospital; if she's needed in the wards again, she might be able to take a peek at Maribeth's chart. But that will help only if she can read the doctor's handwriting, which makes it a very long shot.'' Joanie went into the kitchen and opened the refrigerator. The path must have been fraught with inspiration, because when she returned with a beer, she said, ''Why don't you look at Maribeth's chart at Ultima?''

''Because the information is confidential.''

''And you're going to let that stop you?''

''I can think of someone who might be a tad testy if I were caught breaking and entering,'' I said. ''His thumbscrews may be broken, but his temper's intact.''

Footsteps thudded up the stairs and Caron and Inez flung themselves into the living room. ''Hi, Mrs. Powell,'' Caron said, then looked at me and in a grand display of breathlessness, demanded, ''Guess what, Mother? It's such an Incredible Coincidence that you'll never believe it!''

''Yeah,'' Inez said, merely breathing.

''There's an aerobics class at the youth center? All your friends want to sign up, it costs nothing, it's a short walk, and it's being taught by Jane Fonda?''

''Mother,'' Caron said in a pained whine, but realized her tone was not likely to win friends or influence people vested with maternal authority. ''The classes at the youth center are impossible. We talked to the woman who teaches them, and she said most of the participants are at least sixty years old and like to work out to ancient stuff like big band music. She's probably forty herself—which isn't that old, of course. I mean, you're almost forty and . . . you look okay. . . .'' She paused to consider how to undo the damage.

Inez tiptoed to the rescue. ''We found out about a really neat class just for teens, where they play heavy metal and hard rock. The instructor's young and bouncy, and she says it'll be so exciting to have us join the class.''

''But it's not offered through the youth center, so it's not cheap, it's not conveniently close, and it's not being taught by Jane Fonda. Correct?''

''Correct,'' Caron said, ''but we positively can't waltz with a bunch of old people. This class is designed especially for our age group, and the instructor is a physical education major who studies bones and joints and stuff.' '

"How much does it cost?" I asked mildly.

Caron draped herself across a chair. "I didn't ask, but the first two classes are complimentary, so I don't see why you won't let us try it this week. The class meets at six o'clock for an hour, twice a week. We can go tomorrow, and all you have to do is take us and pick us up."

"Is that all? Can't your mother drive one way, Inez?"

Inez shuffled her feet like a toddler in need of a potty. "She has a meeting tomorrow night. The Budgie Fanciers Club."

Caron snorted. "What's a budgie, some kind of nickname for a budget? Sounds like a really exciting time, figuring out how to pay the rent and keep the children in shoes."

I shushed Caron and gazed at Joanie. "I suppose I might drive them to this class tomorrow evening. I could find somewhere to wait for them, couldn't I?"

"You mean we can go?" Caron shrieked, forgetting about the rent and unclad toes. "Come on, Inez; let's call Rhonda. She'll absolutely die when she hears about this." She started for her room, then stopped and looked back at me. "Could I have a small advance on my allowance? Please? I just know everybody will wear the latest style in leotards, and all I've got are gym shorts and a T-shirt. I don't want to look like some pitiful orphan in Salvation Army used clothes."

"How would you like to live at the Salvation Army shelter?" I countered sweetly. I maintained the smile until her bedroom door slammed closed.

I stayed in bed the next day, partly out of delayed deference to the doctor's orders and partly because the previous day's activities had rekindled a few tiny sparks. I amused myself by calling Luanne Bradshaw, an old friend who'd agreed to babysit the Book Depot for a few days. After a mere three or four calls, she heartlessly announced she would no longer answer the telephone. Maribeth's condition had not changed. The temperature was sixty-three and the time 9:05—and

10:57, 11:14, etc. My accountant was in Hawaii; I took comfort in the knowledge that had he financed his trip by embezzling my money, he would have run out of funds in Muskogee, Oklahoma. Peter was out on a case and Jorgeson had called in sick. The desk sergeant said his grandchildren were fine but that he needed to take more urgent calls. I couldn't think of any Lieutenant Columbo-type questions to hurl at anyone, à la "One more thing, Gerald, why did the potassium caplets turn green under fluorescent light?"

I was actually glad to see Caron and Inez, although Caron was quite the martyred orphan in her shorts and T-shirt. If Inez owned a fashionable leotard, she had enough sense not to wear it and was clad in similar rags.

I opted to drive, and we arrived at Delano's Fitness Center shortly before six o'clock. The door of the Ultima Center had been replaced with a sheet of plywood and the sign hung at a crooked angle, but it seemed it was business as usual, because two clients came out as I parked. I told the girls to go inside the fitness center, then went to the plywood door and, after a stern mental lecture to my trembling hand, opened it and forced myself to enter.

The glass that had comprised the front wall of the office was gone, although the counter, silk flowers, and clipboard were in place. Bobbi Rodriqeuez looked up from a stack of folders. "Hi, Ms. Malloy. Can I help you?"

"I'm surprised you're open."

"It's been one headache after another, for sure, but we have an obligation to our clients. Some of them are in really crucial stages of the program, and we couldn't let them down by closing the center and returning their fees, even if we prorated them."

"Heavens no," I said dryly. "I was hoping I might have a brief look at Maribeth's file, Bobbi. She's still in the coma, and I think there might be something in the file that might explain certain things."

"But it's confidential," Bobbi said, her eyes wide with astonishment.

"She wouldn't mind, especially if it improved her condition.'' I leaned over the counter and studied the name tags on the pile of folders. ''Isn't that hers near the bottom? If you'll let me have ten seconds with it, I swear that no one will ever find out and you'll have helped Maribeth.''

Bobbi nibbled on her lip, then frowned at her wristwatch and said, ''Oh, gee, look how late it is! I'm going to run back and change into my leotard and tights. Would you please wait here in case some late client shows up?'' With the expression of a novitiate on the way to vespers, she left the office through the back door.

I grabbed Maribeth's folder and opened it. The top forms involved liability should the party of the second part suffer any ill effects from the program offered by the party of the first part. Her daily record noted the date of each consultation, weight status, ketone level, and blood pressure. The last recorded visit had been the day of the accident, obviously, and the notation indicated she'd gained a pound, putting her at a running total of minus fourteen. Her blood pressure had gone up. Her weight loss had been consistent and occasionally dramatic for the first twelve days, but after that she lost no more than half a pound a day, and as often gained weight.

I flipped the record aside to read her history, which contained nothing more exotic than mundane childhood diseases, a tonsillectomy, and an allergy to ragweed. All the other boxes in the No column were checked, from appendectomy (give date) through whooping cough.

Disappointed, I looked for the results of the EKG and the blood work ordered when she first enrolled. I found myself looking at the back cover of the folder. I shuffled through the loose pages once again, but I'd seen all there was to see, and I was sliding the folder back into the pile when Bobbi came back to the office, now wearing a shiny black leotard with a diagonal scarlet stripe, matching tights, wristbands, and a headband. She paused to allow me to admire the overall effect, and said, ''Ooh, I've got to lock up this minute and go next door. We have a teen class now, and it's so much fun. The girls just can't get enough; sometimes they even wear

me out by the end of the class.'' She herded me out to the
sidewalk, took a key from her purse, and locked the door
behind us. ''Did you find what you needed in Maribeth's
folder?''

''No,'' I said, still perplexed. ''I thought Ultima did blood
work and an EKG on every client, but I couldn't find any
records in Maribeth's folder.''

Bobbi waved at a group of girls going into the fitness center, then gave me an uncomfortable smile. ''It's part of the
program, but, you see, Dr. Winder and Candice had to use
all their capital, down to the last penny, to lease the building
and put in the examination rooms and remodel and everything. They were using the current fees to finance the EKG
machine and the lab equipment, but none of it arrives until
the middle of next month. Until then, we've been requesting
that clients have the tests done by their personal physicians
and give us copies for the file. That way we know clients
don't have any medical problems that might cause them to
be unsuitable for the program.''

''Did Maribeth do this?''

''She said she'd had the tests done, but she kept forgetting
to bring us the copies. Candice and I reminded her almost
every time she came in for a consultation, and she always
promised she would. But then she'd walk through the door
empty-handed every darn time. It was kind of a joke in the
office.'' She looked at her watch again, squealed, and said,
''Bye now, Ms. Malloy. The girls are probably going nuts to
get started.''

She trotted into the fitness center, leaving me on the sidewalk to wonder why Maribeth had been so determined to
forget her test results. One very logical answer came to mind:
she hadn't been able to afford the tests and was frightened to
ask Gerald for the cash. It was so overwhelmingly logical
that I went over to my car and sat down (very gingerly) on
the hood, mentally patting myself (very softly) on the back.

It was a pleasant evening, the temperature mild and the
street quieting down now that the good citizens of Farberville
were home for dinner. Except for my car, the parking lot in

front of Ultima was empty, and only a few cars were parked in front of Jody's place of business. The windows of the offices beyond were dark, and the spaces in front of them also empty, except for one lone car at the far end. In my balmy philosophical mood, it struck me that no matter how late the hour or remote the parking lot, there is always at least one car parked in every lot.

I squinted at this one but could see no one inside it. A dead battery? A worried owner, holed up in a back room with the accounts? A secretary who'd stayed late and was now being rewarded with dinner before being returned to her car and admonished to drive safely? A burglar casing what I thought was either a chiropractor's office or a family dental center? I wasn't sure what one would steal from a chiropractor, but dentists' offices were stocked with controlled drugs for pain and that wily gas that makes root canals so hilarious.

I was having so much fun I almost slid off the hood when a voice said, "Claire?"

"Yes," I said cautiously, staring at a red eye glowing in the shadow of the building.

Jody Delano came forward, took a final draw on his cigarette, and flipped it into the parking lot. "I didn't intend to startle you. I have to sneak outside for a cigarette, just like when I was a kid in junior high, because the fitness freaks would be harder on me than my old man ever was. He couldn't say much. Emphysema. What are you doing out here?"

"My daughter and a friend are trying the teen class. I'm not a heavy metal fan, so I thought it prudent to wait outside. How are they doing?"

He gave me a crooked grin. "The two wearing T-shirts and shorts? They may be in deeper than they bargained for; Bobbi goes bonkers with this group, and they don't get a break for sixty minutes straight." He took the pack from his pocket, took out another cigarette, and lit it. "I called the hospital before I came outside," he said. "I wish to hell they could do something for Maribeth. I'm sick of this crap about guarded conditions and monitoring vital signs. Why can't they wake her up somehow?''

"I'm sure they would if they could," I said gently. "You two seem to have become close friends since she started coming here so often."

"She always gave it her best. There were plenty of times I'd warn her to slow down, take it easier, walk instead of jog, but she wouldn't pay any attention. Her face'd turn redder than a beet and she'd sound like a steam engine going up a mountainside."

"Shouldn't you have insisted she stop?"

"Naw, the Ultima people are supposed to make sure everyone in the fatties' class is okay. 'Course, most of them didn't work like Maribeth. Sometimes we'd sit in the Jacuzzi until she felt strong enough to get dressed by herself." He threw the cigarette down and ground it out with his heel. "Now she can't do anything for herself, damn it! For all those overeducated, underbrained doctors know, she'll be in a coma for years and years, while her bloodsucking husband enjoys her family's money. He'll have himself a big time, screwing everything with a crotch, drinking champagne on first-class flights to Paris, buying a snooty law firm so they'll have to put his name on the stationery."

His words were passionate enough, but I kept hearing the same siding salesman pitching the same once-in-a-lifetime special. "What would you do in Gerald's position?" I asked.

"I'd sure as hell make sure they did everything possible to bring Maribeth out of the coma. There's probably some clinic in Switzerland that has a miracle cure." He ran his hand through his hair, stared at the darkening sky, then nudged my arm and gave me a comradely wink. "But who's to say, after I'd done everything possible for Maribeth, that I might not have a little fun. But I'd be discreet about it, so that if she woke up, she wouldn't hear any ugly gossip about her old man fooling around."

"One of these days she'll wake up and make a decision," I murmured. "The day of the accident she implied there would be some major changes in her life."

"Did she say anything about me?"

"No, she talked about finishing her degree, then perhaps traveling or opening an art gallery. Should she have said something about you?"

His teeth glinted in the darkness, but I couldn't tell if he smiled or sneered. He lit another cigarette, discarded the matchbook, and blew a column of smoke into the sky. "Naw. I just thought she might have. I've gotten fond of the girl. She's kinda helpless and clumsy, and her husband didn't help, neither. She told me how he used to bring home all this fattening food and leave it all over the house so no matter where she looked it was candy or cookies or cake. He was doing it on purpose, too. I wouldn't treat her like that. No, sir, Joseph Delano wouldn't treat his woman like that."

Once again I could hear the promise of a maintenance-free exterior for life. "Did she seem upset the last week or so about her difficulty in sticking to the program?"

There was a long silence, during which he presumably was collecting his thoughts. I warned myself to wait patiently, in that he was using a sieve at best. At last he let out a lungful of smoke, and in a pensive voice said, "Ya know, she was kind of upset, now that I think about it. There she was, going up and down like a yo-yo, and lying about it, telling everybody she was shedding pounds faster than a snake sheds its skin. I knew she wasn't doing so hot 'cause I'd catch her weighing herself on the scales in the weight room and looking gloomy about it."

"She had me fooled," I said truthfully. "Even with the radical mood swings, she sounded as if she believed she'd lost seventeen pounds the day of the accident. But according to her records, it was fourteen, with a half-pound gain the day before. I suppose she was nibbling at night."

"Damn husband's fault." He pulled out yet another cigarette, fumbled in his pocket, and said, "Be back in a minute; Bobbi's probably got some matches in her purse. Her boyfriend smokes more than I do, if you can buy that."

When he opened the door, the music roared out like the sweeping fiery wind that leveled Hiroshima. I was still reel-

ing when the door again opened briefly, then closed, merci-
fully cutting off the music. Jody rejoined me, and when he'd
lit the cigarette, said, "Those two girls of yours are sitting
on the floor, fanning themselves and looking miserable. They
might do well to start in a low-level class, like the one you
came to at four-thirty with Maribeth several weeks ago.
You're welcome to come with them."

"Thanks; I'll keep it in mind," I lied smoothly.

"If you want, I can give you a deal on a family package
that'll entitle you to use the toning machines. I got to make
some calls now and stuff, but I'll look forward to seeing
you."

I made a vague noise. As he opened the door, I heard
Bobbi yelling, "Go for it! Higher! Harder!"

Caron and Inez staggered out half an hour later and collapsed into the car. "I wanna go home," Caron said in a
hollow voice. Inez repeated the sentiment in a mumble.

"Did we have fun?" I asked as we drove across the parking lot. The car at the far end was still there; as we passed
it, I noticed it was the red sports car I'd seen earlier and that
the surly man, most likely Bobbi's boyfriend, was still surly.
He did not smile. I did not wave.

"Yeah, it was real fun," Caron said. "It was like we'd
been dropped into a boot camp for Marine cheerleaders.
Everyone else thought it was so much fun to do hundreds of
sit-ups and jog in place for hours. You should have heard the
shrieks and squeals. It was disgusting."

"You'll get used to it after a few months of classes," I
said with an evil smile. Neither responded, but I'd had enough
fun and allowed them to subside into muffled groans and
sighs.

My two days of mandatory bed rest were over the following day, and the Book Depot looked very good, although the
overall decor was dustier and my office more chaotic than I
remembered. I waltzed around with a feather duster, thumbed
through a bunch of boring correspondence, and had a futile
telephone conversation with a woman in the distributor's of-

fice who insisted I was in Arizona, which coincidentally was where the shipment of books was.

All the while, however, I kept thinking about Maribeth and her untimely heart attack. She was overweight and therefore at risk, but supposedly she'd had an EKG and blood work before she began the Ultima program. After the fainting episode she'd said she didn't have a local doctor anymore. Had she lied to Candice and Bobbi—or had she lied to Peter and me?

The previous evening I was certain she wasn't able to have the tests for financial reasons, but now I began to wonder if there might be another reason, one that involved the unspecified problem in college that forced her to drop out of school. I doubted I could ring up the college infirmary and ask about medical records from seven or eight years ago, especially since I didn't know the name of the college and was bereft of credentials. Gerald didn't seem to know, or at least didn't seem inclined to tell me.

Maribeth had mentioned a pediatrician, although she'd said he was ancient when she was a child. It occurred to me that he might have been aware of some medical condition that might have led to the college problem and even the heart attack. Children tend to view all adults over forty as ancient, over fifty as senile, and over sixty as ambulatory dead. If I could find the pediatrician, I might be able to persuade him to discuss any conditions from her childhood. A big if.

I took out the telephone book and ascertained there were only ten pediatricians in Farberville, the majority of them divided between two clinics. I contemplated the wisdom of calling each and demanding to know how old he or she was, but I decided the approach was less than tactful and waited impatiently until Caron and Inez dragged themselves into the store after school. It was their least dramatic entrance to date; I usually clutched the nearest inanimate object to steady myself when they exploded into my presence.

"Feeling a little sore?" I asked.

"Not at all," Caron said with a telltale wince. She came around the counter to the stool and climbed on to it with a muted moan. "I lost three pounds and I feel great. Don't you feel great, Inez?"

"Me, too, and I feel great," Inez echoed obediently.

"I need you to watch the store until closing," I said. "I'm going to visit all the local pediatricians." They were both gaping at me as I left, but I couldn't think of a plausible lie and I didn't have time for the truth.

At the first office I asked to speak to the resident physician and was told she was at the hospital. One down, nine to go. The second office was packed with runny-nosed toddlers, bawling babies, and devilish children beating on each other with wooden toys. As I approached the reception window, a young man with a stethoscope around his neck and dressed in a white coat splattered with vomit stomped into the inner office and snatched up a folder. Too young.

Four of the pediatricians were at the first clinic. I went to the window and politely inquired if any of them had been in practice twenty years ago. The receptionist looked at me as if I'd asked if any of them had orange and black striped tails.

"My child is ill," I improvised blandly, "and I think she might be more comfortable with a grandfatherly type."

"Where's the sick child?"

"She's . . . in the car, getting sicker by the second. Would you please tell me if any of the pediatricians are elderly?"

It was obvious she felt as though she was dealing with a demented psychotic stalking senior members of the medical profession. "We have a separate waiting room for sick children," she said, then added loudly enough to be heard at the nearest SCAN office, "Do you really think a sick child ought to be left alone in the car?"

All the mothers in the waiting room turned to stare darkly at me, as did an eagle-beaked nurse armed with a clipboard. "Oh, she can't reach the gas pedal," I said with a gay laugh. "But little Beatrice goes wild with fear unless she has a doctor who reminds her of dear old Granddaddy. She screams like a banshee, wets her pants, and begins to throw up. However, if you want to risk it . . ."

The receptionist regarded me for a long minute, making it clear she didn't believe a word of my story and was quite sure I had an ax in my purse. "Our physicians are all in their mid to late thirties," she said at last, "and would feel dreadful if they were the cause of little Beatrice's hysterics."

A young doctor wearing Mickey Mouse ears appeared from a corner of the office and said, "There aren't any older pediatricians in Farberville. Too bad my father's not practicing; he was seventy-three when he retired."

"Could I speak to you in private?" I said. "It's rather complicated, but it's important."

"For a moment." He beckoned to a nearby nurse. "The Kerossack child is waiting for inoculations in room four. Use the straps if necessary, but this time nail him and nail him good. Little darling bit me again."

He escorted me to his office and sat down behind his desk. "You've got a semihysterical sick child in the car, but you want to speak to me, right?"

I fumbled around in my mind, then took a deep breath and gave him an accurate if abridged explanation for my purpose in hunting down elderly pediatricians. "If I could have a word with your father, it might clear up some of this muddle," I concluded with a beguiling smile.

"My father was the only pediatrician in Farberville twenty years ago, although a lot of families preferred to use a general practitioner. As I said earlier, he retired when he was seventy-three. I failed to add that he died when he was seventy-five."

"Damn," I muttered, then hastily said, "Sorry, I thought I'd finally made some progress. The comatose girl's only twenty-nine, and she was beginning to truly enjoy life when the accident occurred."

He made a pyramid with his fingers and studied me for a long while. "Dad's records are stored in my garage. Give me the patient's name and I'll see if I can find her file."

I scribbled Maribeth's maiden name, my name, my home telephone number, and the number at the Book Depot. I thanked him profusely and went to my car, but as I drove home I realized I was clinging to a very thin thread. If I had found the right pediatrician, and if he'd saved Maribeth's childhood records, and if there was anything significant in them, then . . . what?

I regret to say that nothing much came to mind, and I drove home in an increasingly glum mood. I collected my mail and started to go upstairs, then halted and knocked on Joanie's door.

She waved me in and said, "I asked my daughter if she knew anything about Maribeth's problem in college, but she didn't. Betty Lou's not scheduled to volunteer any time this week. I'm not much of a sleuth, I'm afraid, but I do have fresh coffee and homemade cookies."

I shook my head and sank down on a love seat. "I may be on the track of Maribeth's pediatrician, but I'm not sure that whatever information I get, presuming I get any, will be pertinent. What we need is motive and opportunity, not a dusty medical history."

"Isn't the husband always the most popular suspect?" Joanie said.

"He's got opportunity. Maribeth most likely kept her vitamins in a kitchen cabinet or in the bathroom; he could have substituted something. He's not fond of Maribeth, but he is exceedingly fond of her trust fund, and he wouldn't want to murder her before she came into the money."

"Lust can make people lose sight of more practical considerations. Could he have been so enamored of Candice that he was willing to do anything to rid himself of his wife?"

"Then all he had to do was divorce her," I said, sinking further into both the upholstery and despair. "If he wouldn't do so because of all the lovely money, Candice might have been motivated to take action, and she had ample opportunity to switch the potassium caplets for placebos of some kind. Damn, I wish the CID had run tests on the bottle of potassium."

Joanie went into her kitchen and returned with a beer, a bottle of scotch, two glasses, and a glazed expression. "But," she said pensively, "Candice met with Maribeth five afternoons a week for their consultation and weigh-in, and I'd imagine she was aware that Maribeth was developing a sense of independence as she gained control of her life. All she had to do was encourage Maribeth to continue with the program and then wait for her to dump Gerald.''

"Maribeth wasn't making much progress the third week," I said. I described the contents of the daily record, then added, "Maybe Candice panicked and decided to take matters into her own hands. Pretty feeble, huh?''

"No more than my son's excuses for overdrawing his bank account," Joanie said with a sniff. "It's odd, though. Maribeth told me she was losing steadily, yet she must have known otherwise. I'm surprised that she would lie to either of us.''

"If she was lying, she was doing it well. After all the years with Caron, I'm not the most trusting person on the planet, but I believed Maribeth, too," I admitted. "Candice knew otherwise, as did Jody Delano. Yesterday he told me Maribeth weighed herself on his scales at the fitness center, I suppose to confirm the figures from the Ultima Center.''

"Is there any way he could be involved?''

I shrugged. "I don't see how. He was panting after Maribeth, not trying to get rid of her. He may be perfectly sincere, or, like Gerald, he may have his eye on the trust money, but in either case he has no motive. He could hardly fiddle with the bottles of potassium in the office, for that matter. Even if he did, he had no control over which bottle was given to Maribeth. The other Ultima clients don't seem to have any of the symptoms we saw in Maribeth's case; they have a predatory look about them, not unlike vultures, but they're not snarling or fainting or entering the Ultima office through a drive-in window.''

"That leaves Sheldon Winder and Bobbi," Joanie said morosely. "Neither has any reason to try to harm Maribeth.''

"Unless . . .'' I stared at the wall above Joanie's head. When she made an irritated rumble, I said, "Well, what if Shelly and Bobbi are having a mad affair? It isn't all that unlikely. The evening I stopped by to talk to him, he was up to something with a mysterious client in one of the back rooms. He claimed it was someone who was embarrassed to come in during regular hours, but he was, as my grandmother used to say at every opportunity until the entire family wanted to throttle her, as nervous as a long-tailed cat in a roomful of rocking chairs. Maybe he made the crack about unnatural sex at the funeral to throw us off.''

"So they're having an affair. So what?"

"If it had reached epic intensity, one or the other might decide to get rid of Maribeth in order to make Gerald available. Then Candice would sacrifice her interest in the Ultima Center to expedite a divorce in order to marry him. Then they could get married, too. For all we know, Bobbi may have nurtured a girlish dream of a double ceremony. I admit I'm stretching, but if we're presuming someone wanted Maribeth out of the way, then we're going to have to stretch like a pair of queen-sized panty hose.''

A tap at the door stopped further speculation. Caron stood in the hallway, her lower lip thrust forward and her eyes narrowed. "I came downstairs to give you a message," she said to me accusingly. "I saw you drive up, but I presumed you'd come upstairs out of consideration for Other People, who might be tired of walking up and down the stairs all day long.''

"What's the message?" I asked.

"The guy had to spell it out so I could write it down. It took me five minutes to find a pencil." She handed the paper to Joanie and stomped upstairs, conveying disapproval with each thud.

Joanie frowned at the smudged note. " 'Acute rheumatic fever, carditis, antibiotic therapy. Age ten. Hope Beatrice is better.' What does this mean, Claire? Who's Beatrice?"

"Beatrice is a malevolent child inclined to tantrums. What's important is that Maribeth had rheumatic fever as

TEN

The following morning, after Caron had wolfed down a large breakfast (in order to increase endurance and build muscle tissue, I was told huffily), and then filled her purse with cookies (quick energy and blood sugar, huff, huff) and left for school, I called the CID and asked for Lieutenant Rosen.

After we'd exchanged pleasantries, I said, "Are you aware that Maribeth Galleston had rheumatic fever as a child, and a relapse of some kind while in college?"

"I am. Are you aware you're once again meddling in official police business?"

"I'm doing no such thing," I said, offended at the very idea. "You're the one who said the case was closed, that the CID was no longer interested in the so-called accident. You couldn't be bothered to run tests on the potassium or find out who was having affairs with whom. You're more interested in football players taking illegal substances to make their biceps bulge and their triceps triple."

He grumbled for a moment, then said, "I told you that in confidence, and then asked you to butt out of the Galleston investigation. It is closed. Hold a vigil beside her bed at the hospital, send her flowers, read her one of those fanciful mystery novels in which the busybody amateur sleuth outwits the plodding policeman, or, if none of that appeals, mind your own business.''

''Why didn't you tell me about the rheumatic fever?'' I inserted, tiring of the drift of his remarks. ''Do you realize what I went through to get that bit of information? I'm apt to come down with chicken pox or diaper rash, all because you couldn't bother to mention it to me.''

''Claire,'' he said in a drawn-out sigh, ''it's against department policy to keep civilians informed of our every move. If we didn't prefer a little privacy, we'd issue bulletins every evening on the six o'clock news.''

I blinked at the receiver. ''You would?''

''I'm joking.''

''I know that. It's just that . . .'' I blinked once more, then told myself to stop being foolish. ''Did you find out anything about Sheldon and Candice Winder?''

''Nothing of great interest. He went to medical school in Guadalajara, but a lot of Americans do, when they can't get accepted anywhere else. He finagled an internship at a small hospital but was terminated during the first year. Shortly thereafter he proclaimed himself an expert in the field of nutrition and weight problems and opened the Ultima Center.''

''Why was he terminated?''

''It took some digging; the profession's closedmouthed about its malpractitioners. Winder was supposed to be on call one night, but he was occupied handily in the linen closet with a winsome nurse. There was an emergency; the patient requiring attention died. The director was irked enough to kick Winder out of the program, but not enough to disturb the licensing board.''

''The nurse being Candice?''

''Yes, and she received the same treatment. One of her more garrulous roommates said Candice was hot to marry a doctor, even one with uncertain earning power. She demanded Winder marry her to justify the grand passion that led to her termination and badgered him continually until he gave in.''

''And ended up in a diet center, fawning over obese women and shrieking with glee when one of them lost a pound.''

''So it seems.'' Peter then said he had to go play with his police band radio and I said I needed to mind my own business: the bookstore. I replaced the receiver and tried to find a spot in the puzzle for the latest tidbits of information. Winder was a lousy doctor. Candice was not my choice of Nightingales. If she'd grown tired of her husband, she might have set her black-striped cap for Gerald. Who would refuse to divorce his heiress. Who was terrified she might divorce him. Who would prefer to have his heiress committed. Who might have mentioned as much to Candice, who obligingly suggested a plan. They couldn't kill her, but they could arrange for her to become increasingly incapable of normal functioning. Once she was stashed for life, they could do almost everything except marry each other.

I went downstairs and knocked on Joanie's door. When she opened it, I said, ''Will you call Betty Lou Kirkpatrick and find out the name of her law-professor daughter, then call the daughter and ask when there's a faculty meeting or whatever where attendance is mandatory?''

''I have to fire in ten minutes.''

''A gun? An employee? Off a memo?''

''I have to fire a particularly exquisite hand-built vase, Claire, and you're blocking the doorway. I'm going to have to run across campus as it is, and it won't be a pretty picture. Why don't you call Betty Lou and ask all those things?''

''I don't know her. Can you call her after you've fired the vase?'' I persisted.

''I'll catch Betty Lou later in the morning and call you at the Book Depot.'' She gave me a shrewd look. ''Shall I pass the vase to raise bail?''

''Good idea. Remember to remove the money before you fire it.''

I walked to the Book Depot and called the hospital to check on Maribeth. Her condition had not changed. I sold a few books, agreed to order one not in stock, paced up and down the aisles, and finally snatched up the feather duster to vent my impatience on Chaucer, Dante, and the rest of the freshman lit gang. I was so edgy that I nearly knocked down a customer when I glanced up and saw a face peering through the window. The disembodied head disappeared, but it cost me a sale and a goodly amount of professional pride. As a rule, proprietors try to avoid scaring off customers. Plays havoc with sales.

I picked out a self-help on stress-related disorders, sat on the stool behind the counter, and waited for Joanie's call. By noon I was reduced to glowering at the telephone, and I almost shrieked when it rang.

Pleased by my psychic powers, I grabbed the receiver and said, "Did you get through to Betty Lou?"

"Any relation to Peggy Sue?" Peter answered, humming a few bars so I could fully appreciate his quick wit.

"No, it's . . . someone who goes to basketball games. Joanie was going to see if I could use her ticket for the next game."

"In two months, when basketball season opens? How clever of you to plan ahead so carefully."

I scowled at the receiver, but in a properly modulated voice, said, "Thank you. It's been lovely chatting with you, but I'm waiting for Joanie to call and it's rather urgent."

"I know how fond you are of basketball. Listen, I'm going to violate department regulations to share—voluntarily, mind you—some information about the Galleston case."

"You are?"

"I'm doing this so you'll stop nosing around, Claire. The tests done at the hospital turned up a certain amount of heart damage from childhood rheumatic fever. Maribeth shouldn't have been on a stringent diet, but she shouldn't have suffered any serious complications from it as long as she took all the vitamins and supplements prescribed. Apparently she didn't; we found three bottles of potassium caplets in a kitchen cabinet, and they were unopened."

"Did you test them to see if they really were potassium?" I asked politely . . . for the third or fourth time.

"Yes, they had been packaged for Ultima and consisted of precisely what the label described. The truth is that for some unknown reason she wasn't taking them, and that led to the dizziness and vagueness."

"Oh," I said, somewhat sad to see my lovely theory deflate. "Then the self-induced potassium deficiency was responsible for everything, from the outbursts to the heart attack? Maribeth simply didn't follow the program, and it resulted in her coma and Candice's death?"

"That's right," Peter said. He wished me luck getting basketball tickets on the fifty-yard line and hung up.

I kept the receiver in my hand, staring at it as I replayed the conversation in my mind. Everything had sounded fine until I'd mentioned the outbursts and the heart attack. And heard the damn omnipresent siding salesman once again.

I found the telephone directory, called the pediatric clinic, and asked to speak to the helpful young doctor with the big black ears.

"He's with a patient. Do you need to make an appointment?"

"No, I need to speak to him for a minute. Maybe not even that long. Thirty seconds. Forty-five, tops."

"If you'll give me the child's name, your number, and the nature of the child's illness, I'll have Dr. Brandisi's nurse call you when she's free."

"I need to speak to him personally."

"Is this Beatrice's mother?" the voice said so coldly I could almost see icicles forming on telephone wires across the city.

"No," I said truthfully, "my child's name is Caron."

"And what is the nature of Caron's illness?"

"Usually it's mental, but these days I'm wondering if she's developing an eating disorder. Last week she insisted on nothing but popcorn and grapefruit juice for most of a day. Could I please speak to Dr. Brandisi?"

"If you'll give me your name and telephone number, I'll

put a note on his desk. However, his schedule is very, very busy, and he won't be able to call until late in the afternoon.''

After I'd rattled off the information and repeated several times that I wanted to speak to Dr. Brandisi personally, I hung up and resumed pacing. Peter's call was peculiar; unlike Betty Lou, he did not volunteer anything, including information from his investigation. Furthermore, it didn't make any more sense than my muddled theories that someone had tampered with the potassium. Maribeth had no reason not to take the potassium. Sighing loudly enough to startle the roaches, I reminded myself that she didn't have a reason to lie about her progress, either—but she had.

I finally gave up on Joanie, put the CLOSED sign on the Book Depot door, and walked back to my apartment for lunch. I went halfway up the stairs, stopped, went back down and around to the garage and got into my car, although I wasn't quite sure where I was going.

By the time I reached the street, I'd figured out that I was going to the Ultima Center to have a word with Sheldon Winder. Which word remained to be seen, but I was decidedly unhappy with the tidy conclusion to the untidy mess. I preferred my conspiracy theory; Winder might find something in the daily record to confirm it.

As I drove down the hill beside the football stadium, I was smiling at the image of Peter and the feds skulking under the bleachers, armed not with deadly assault weapons but with little glass bottles. The stadium was empty, as was the practice field below it; I supposed the players were obliged to attend a class or two in the morning. Some of them, no doubt, shared Bobbi's classes in joints and ankles, along with demanding courses in recreational opportunities, recruitment violations (Evasion 101), and athletic department budget management.

The car ahead of me slowed and its blinker began to imply a turn was imminent. I agreeably put my foot on the brake pedal. The pedal hit the floor. My emergency brake had ceased working several years ago. I would have pumped the brake pedal, but it remained flat against the floorboard. All the while my car was picking up speed on the steep slope. I whipped around the right side of the car ahead of me, only to be confronted with the brake lights of a pickup truck. No one was coming toward us in the other lane. I passed the truck on the left and swung back to the proper side. Fighting an inexplicable urge to giggle, I eyed the next challenge—a lumbering white garbage truck. In that there was a convert- ible in the left lane, I couldn't pass on that side. On the right was a slight valley and an upward incline with a few scattered trees and a stern sign to those who might entertain the idea of parking on the grass.

I wrenched the wheel to the right, bounced over the curb (bouncing my head off the top of the car hard enough to bring an instant gush of tears and an expletive of Anglo-Saxon origin), veered around a tree, sucked in a breath, and veered around yet another tree. I tried to downshift, but the gears squealed so painfully I could almost see the teeth being stripped. I felt as though I had been dropped inside a mani- acal video game, but the trees were very three-dimensional and my thudding heart very much in my throat.

I was on an upward incline now. If I could avoid a few more impediments, the car would yield to the laws of gravity. I did not avoid a metal trash receptacle, but I missed three more trees and eventually, after a mere eternity, came to rest two feet from a concrete picnic table.

As I cut off the engine, the giggles caught up with me. I leaned my forehead on the steering wheel, tears forming in my eyes, and tried to combat what I sensed was impending hysterics. My heart eventually sank back into its proper cav- ity. The shrill giggles gave way to moist hiccups. My breath- ing steadied, and my shoulders stopped jerking as if an electric current was running through them.

A rap on the window interrupted my internal assessment. I turned my head and gazed blankly at a man in stained overalls and a baseball cap. He twirled his finger until I rolled down the window. "No parking on the grass, ma'am," he said, pointing with his thumb at a nearby sign.

"I'm not parking."

"Looks like parking to me, ma'am. Your car's on the grass. Planning a little picnic?"

"There's something wrong with my brake pedal. It went all the way to the floorboard without slowing me down. I managed to avoid an accident by coming this way." Wondering if my knees could be trusted, I opened the car door and managed a wobbly posture on the violated grass. "Look for yourself."

He bent down over the driver's seat for a moment, then stood up and said, "Yeah, the pedal's down there, all right. You still can't park here, ma'am. The mower's coming pretty soon."

"Why would the pedal give way like that?" I said, frowning. "It was fine last night."

"How should I know? I'm not a mechanic. All I know is that you're not allowed to park here and the mower's coming pretty soon. If you want me to call campus security on my walkie-talkie, I will. But in the meantime—"

"I can't park here," I interrupted with a wan smile. "Then again, I can't drive away without brakes, can I? That might result in a problem at some point in the immediate future, if I need to slow down or even to stop. If you'll direct me to the nearest telephone, I'll call a tow truck."

"Probably in the administration building at the top of the hill there. There's a pay phone in the hall, I think. But what am I supposed to do when the mower comes? I think I'd better notify campus security and let them deal with this."

I took my purse from the car, found a ten-dollar bill, and held it delicately between thumb and forefinger. "Let's not disturb the security men. I suggest the mower mow around the car until a tow truck arrives. Do you think that might be possible?"

It was possible. I trudged up the hill to the gray administration building, located the pay phone, waited impatiently while a dithery blond coed cooed to an unseen admirer, and eventually arranged for a tow service to collect my car from underneath the jaws of the mower and repair the brake pedal. I didn't gasp at the amount of money required for all this, but I was hardly smiling as I replaced the receiver and leaned against the wall.

Coincidences might be the mainstay of fiction, but this was reality. My car was fifteen years old; the brakes had never failed before. I'd been snooping around, asking questions, and somewhere along the way I'd pinched a nerve. The cozy notion that someone had tried to stop me caused my knees to weaken and my head to throb. Students swarmed through the hallway, their expressions grim as they prepared to face impersonal, money-hungry secretaries in the bursar's office. I warranted a few incurious glances as I cautiously explored the lump on the top of my head, wincing, and then fought my way out of the building.

I sat on a low brick wall and watched a campus security car drive across the grass and park next to my car. The treacherous maintenance man waved his hands about, clearly explaining the lurid details of the felonious assault on the lawn, and followed the cop to the rear of my car in order to make sure the license plate number was recorded accurately. I was not overcome with surprise; my one previous attempt to bribe someone had turned out no better, since the bribee subsequently was introduced as an undercover cop under orders from Lieutenant Peter Rosen, who'd found it highly diverting.

The security cops left. A few minutes later a tow truck approached my car, coupled itself, and drove away with my only means of transportation. I wasn't especially eager to get behind a steering wheel, but my apartment was on the far side of the campus and I wasn't sure I could survive the hike. Then again, my options were limited and I doubted a limo would stop in front of me, with a solicitous chauffeur who would settle me in back with tea and a dozen aspirin. I forced myself up and trudged down the sidewalk.

When I reached the corner of the library, however, I headed for the fine arts building adjacent to it. The students on the sidewalk wore skirts and blouses or button-down collars and ties (depending on their gender), but the denizens of the fine arts building were . . . artier. Here the long hair was equally divided between genders, as was the cropped, bushy hair, and a scattering of unnatural colors. Ragged jeans and blue cotton work shirts seemed to be the uniform of the day; in that I'd been in college in the sixties, it was more familiar.

I wandered around until I spotted a ponytailed man with the same grayish splatters on his clothes that Joanie favored. I asked him where someone might fire something. Unlike others of us, he resisted an impulse to make feeble jokes and directed me to the pottery labs in the basement rather than to the ROTC firing range.

Joanie was on the bottom step of the stairwell, talking to a girl with orange hair and earrings that dangled to her shoulders.

"I thought you were going to call me," I said sternly.

"Goodness, what are you doing here?" she said. "I tried to call earlier, but no one answered the phone at the store." She shooed the orange person away, then patted the step beside her. "You'd better sit down, Claire; you look worse than last week's casserole."

I did as suggested. "I think someone fiddled with the brakes in my car. I nearly took out half a dozen freshmen and two trucks before I settled for a metal trash can and a chunk of lawn. I'm feeling a little weak about the whole thing."

"Fiddled with the brakes? When?"

"The garage isn't locked, so someone could have done it last night, or even this morning while I was at the store. Maybe I'm being paranoid, but the brakes were fine yesterday and decidedly nonfunctional an hour ago."

"Are you sure it isn't just one of those not-so-funny cosmic jokes, Claire?"

"I'm not sure of anything," I said peevishly, "except that something's going on and I don't like it." I repeated what Peter had told me earlier about the potassium stash in Maribeth's kitchen. "Can you thínk of a reason why she might refuse to take the potassium and then lie about it? When I first met her, she was on a self-destructive track, but her success on the Ultima program and in the exercise classes was doing a great deal to enhance her confidence. Why in hell would she act like that?'' I realized my voice was echoing in the tunnel and ordered myself to calm down. ''Maribeth seemed to be candid with us at first, but according to what I've learned, she was lying through her teeth the week before the accident. I like her, damn it. I don't want to categorize her as a liar.''

''Then don't,'' Joanie said.

''How can I not?'' I said, exasperated. I stood up and began to pace in the narrow hall. ''Peter said she'd stashed the unopened bottles of potassium caplets in the cabinet. She assured me the day she fainted that she'd skipped only two caplets and would be careful not to skip any again. Sheldon said her progress was erratic, and the chart confirmed that, yet she was telling us how well she was doing.''

''Maybe that's what she believed. If Peter's so confident that everything is neatly packaged and ready to file away, then how can he explain the sabotage to your brakes? Maribeth didn't do it.''

I gave her a dark look. ''He can't explain it because he'll never hear about it. The one thing I don't need is one of his tedious, pedantic, suffocating lectures about meddlesome amateurs and efficient professionals. On the other hand, I'm in dire need of a couple of aspirin.''

She took a small tin from her purse, handed me two tablets, and waited in silence while I went to the drinking fountain and choked them down. ''But what if Maribeth has been saying what she perceives to be the truth—that she faithfully took potassium every day and was losing weight steadily?'' she asked me.

If my head hadn't been so sore I would have let out a screech of frustration that would have shattered all the exquisite hand-built vases in the basement. I settled for a muttered, ''That's not possible. How could she not know?''

Joanie glanced at her watch. ''Oh dear, it's time to check the kiln. I've never pretended to be the local version of Miss Marple, Claire; you're the one with that particular claim to fame. I just thought I'd throw out a suggestion or two.''

She was a nice person, and in my heart of hearts I knew I shouldn't strangle her on the spot—despite the urge to do so. "Did you get in touch with Betty Lou?" I said through clenched teeth.

"That's why I tried to call earlier. Betty Lou spoke to her daughter, who reported that there's a cocktail party today at six for a potential faculty member from Chicago . . . or was it Detroit? It seems the daughter has a fabulous house and is usually coerced into holding the functions there. All the faculty members are expected to attend in order to size up the candidate." She again glanced at her watch, twitched like the White Rabbit, and called a farewell over her shoulder as she hurried down the hall.

I went upstairs, out the door, and back to the sidewalk, heading in the direction of my apartment, but even in the sunshine I felt as if I were still in the dark, dreary basement tunnel. Peter presumed Maribeth had lied; Joanie suggested I presume she had told the truth—as she perceived it.

"Peter," I said aloud, startling a trio of fraternity boys on a bench, "has the better argument: the potassium was truly potassium, and the potassium was in bottles rather than where it should have been, which is in Maribeth. The doctor at the hospital said she had a potassium deficiency. Her behavior confirmed his diagnosis."

"You lost, lady?" one of the boys said, snickering.

I certainly felt as if I were, but I shrugged and continued, still mumbling under my breath like an escapee from the banana-nut-bread bakery. "If Maribeth wasn't lying, then she thought she was taking potassium three times a day." I slowed down, and finally stopped in the middle of the sidewalk, ignoring the students forced to step around me. She thought she was taking potassium—but she wasn't. Ergo, she indeed was taking a substitute, as I'd originally hypothesized.

Peter had said tests had been done. However, he'd only told me a few hours ago, which meant the tests weren't necessarily ordered until several days after the accident. Whoever had switched the potassium could have switched it back before the CID had bestirred itself to send the bottles to the lab.

I jarred myself back into motion in time to avoid being trampled by a herd of serenely oblivious sorority girls and hurried to my apartment, feeling very much better. All I had to do was determine who could have made the exchange, and the man who cohabited in the house seemed likely to have access to the cabinet. A bit of proof might be required before I called Peter, I supposed, but I could cross that bridge when or if I ever found myself in the general vicinity of it.

Lunchtime had come and gone by this time, so I grabbed an apple and went back to the Book Depot, hoping this had not been the first time ever that zillions of book buyers had converged on the store, checkbooks bulging, and been confronted with the CLOSED sign. I spent the rest of the afternoon trying to devise a solid case against Gerald and/or Candice, but I had no luck and was merely moping when Caron and Inez came by.

"Are you feeling better?" I asked, determined to sound properly concerned if not totally sympathetic.

"Yeah," Caron muttered, "so I guess we'll go again tonight, although I'm not convinced that Bobbi person knows everything there is to know about joints and stuff. It can't be healthy to jump up and down like a pogo stick for fifteen minutes."

Inez nodded. "Caron and I wondered if it might be bad for our ankles, Mrs. Malloy. But we did lose three pounds each."

"I'd do better if I had a decent leotard," Caron added, studying me for the faintest crack of financial vulnerability.

"Forget it," I said. "There's a minor complication if you're intending for me to drive you to the fitness center tonight. My car's in the shop with brake problems."

Caron glared at me. "Minor? Are we supposed to walk all the way there, jump around for an hour, and then walk home?" When I shrugged, she lapsed into martyrdom and said, "Inez's parents have gone to another pet thing and won't be home until late tonight. I suppose"—a windy sigh—"I

can ask Peter if he can take us. Maybe he'll let me drive his
car.''

"Don't do that," I said. "Let me call the shop and find
out when the car will be ready." I dialed the number, asked
to be put through to the service department, identified myself, and inquired if they had located the brake problem. I
was informed that they had indeed: the cotter pin was missing, which had caused the pivot pin to work loose, which
had caused the brake pedal to collapse against the floorboard.

"The cotter pin," I repeated carefully, although I had no
idea what it might be. "What could cause the cotter pin to
fall out?''

"Nothing. They don't fall out by themselves; they have to
be pulled out with a pair of pliers. There were some scratches
on the pivot pin that looked like someone had done just that.''

Aware of the girls' scrutiny, I swallowed back a few hysterical questions and asked when the car would be available.
The mechanic promised to have it the next morning, and
although he was obviously curious about the pin and the
scratches, I said I'd be there and cut him off in mid-question.

"Joanie should be home by now," I said, trying not to
sound like someone who'd just learned of an attempt on her
life. "I'll see if I can borrow her car and take you to the
aerobics class.'' That would give me most of an hour to go
to the Galleston's house, break and enter, search for potassium caplets that were not potassium caplets, and pick up
the girls. It was a long shot, in that the substituted caplets
most likely had been replaced, but I'd decided earlier that
Maribeth might have left part of a bottle in her bedside drawer
or in her bathroom. Furthermore, it was the only thing I
could think of to do, and I loathe idleness.

"But if Peter took us, I could drive," Caron muttered.

I sent them away with a stern order not to call Peter, then
called Joanie and asked if I could borrow her car to take the
girls to their class at six o'clock.

"Is that the only place you're going?" she said suspi-
ciously.

"It's apt to be the last time I have to take them," I said,

neatly averting the question. "They're entitled to two free classes, and then it costs money. Neither one of them is enjoying the class enough to actually pay for it. They'll decide they've reached their optimum weight, which will be whatever they weigh at the time."

"You're not going to Maribeth's house?"

It was her fault. After Peter's call that morning, I'd abandoned my admittedly screwy plan to search the house, but after her question in the fine arts basement, I'd changed my mind. This convoluted reasoning allowed me to say, "Of course not. Will you be home a little before six?"

"No. I'll leave the car key in your mailbox—if you're quite sure you're not planning anything Peter would disapprove of, Claire."

"Me?" I chuckled at the very idea.

"All right, then, as long as you've promised. I was in such a rush earlier that I didn't tell you what Betty Lou's daughter said about Gerald Galleston."

"You asked her about him? The last thing we need to do is make him suspicious, Joanie."

"I'm aware of that," she said in a haughty voice. "I merely asked if she knew about poor Maribeth Galleston's condition, an innocent question. She said she'd heard something, but that Gerald rarely mentions his wife and never brings her to faculty functions. I was more than discreet; she was the one who offered the information."

"Did she say anything else about Gerald?"

"Only that he may need the Farber trust fund by the end of the spring semester, because his drinking problem is interfering with his academic duties and he's liable to find himself at a cocktail party for his successor." She paused to allow me to make a thoughtful noise. "What's more, she knows one of the trustees of the fund, who told her the approximate amount of money coming to Maribeth. It's in the range of twelve million dollars, give or take a few hundred thousand."

My mouth fell open, and it took me a moment to regain control of it. "Twelve million dollars? I don't know what I thought the figure was, but I think I was underestimating Thurber Farber's business acumen. There are a lot of people who'd steal their grandmother's cotter pin for that kind of money."

"And prefer to be married to an heiress in a coma rather than to one in an attorney's office inquiring about the daily special on divorces. As long as you're not plotting anything illegal, I'll leave the car key for you, but if you're lying, then you can kiss off any hope of an exquisite hand-built vase on your mantel."

"I never lie," I said mendaciously. I thanked her, then hung up and waited until the last moment to lock the store and walk home. Dr. Brandisi had not returned my call, but I wouldn't bet more than a nickel, give or take a few cents, that the receptionist had put my message on his desk. When I reached the duplex, the key was in the mailbox, the girls were in their shorts and T-shirts, and, if all was right with the world, Gerald Galleston was in Betty Lou's daughter's dining room, sipping sherry and hurling trick questions at the candidate.

I dropped the girls off and drove to the Galleston house, which was dark. I parked on the street, but as I approached the gate, a elderly woman in a long overcoat, scarf, and thick-soled shoes came around the corner, or, more accurately, was dragged around the corner by a fierce German shepherd at the end of a leash.

"Are you planning to visit Mrs. Galleston?" the woman chirped. She yanked at the leash and said, "Sit, you filthy animal." She looked back at me, her eyes brightly inquisitive.

I had no idea if the woman knew that Maribeth was in the hospital. "I was just dropping off a few things for her, ah, Avon products she ordered last week."

She took in my empty hands. "Isn't that nice," she said, yanked again on the leash, and trudged ahead. The dog looked back at me, his expression as skeptical as his mistress's.

I felt silly as I walked up the driveway, but I had no time

to run back to the woman and further fray the situation with a garbled explanation. The doorbell rang hollowly, as it had before, and I waited a prudent five minutes before testing the front door. It was locked, a very un-Farberville-ish gesture. The windows along the side of the house were locked, as were the back door and the windows on the other side. According to cop shows and PI novels, all one had to do was slip a credit card into the lock, but I'd left home without it.

It was almost six-thirty; I'd wasted nearly half of my allotted time. The whole scheme was seeming madder by the minute. I returned to the back door and rattled it, then noticed the window above it was open partially. To be precise, the second-story window. Of an older house, with very high ceilings.

There was a ratty shed behind the house, and it looked like a perfect place to keep a ladder. Offering a silent prayer to the god of propitiousness, I yanked open the door and squinted into the dim interior. There were cardboard boxes filled with yellowed newspapers, a stack of tires, a small forest of battered gallon paint cans, several rolls of chicken wire, and in the far corner, a cobweb-coated ladder. It took several sneezes, a bruised shin, a close encounter with a dead mouse, and more than ten minutes to extricate the ladder, but eventually I dragged it to the back of the house and propped it beneath the window.

Trying not to dwell on my aversion to heights, I crawled up the ladder and opened the window wide enough so that I could slither through it. I landed on the floor of what I brilliantly deduced to be a bathroom of nineteenth-century vintage, complete with a bathtub on claws, a rusted gas heater in the wall, and buckling linoleum.

It was as good a place to start as any. I had less than twenty minutes left if I wanted to be at the fitness center at seven o'clock to pick up Caron and Inez, and any inconvenience on their part would be broadcast loudly to anyone who would listen, including Joanie Powell and Super Cop.

The shelves behind the mirrored medicine cabinet contained ancient tubes of toothpaste, an encrusted disposable razor, a book of matches, and a box of Dr. Browning's Digestive Powder. The cabinets below the sink held a toilet brush, a pile of rags, a copy of *Life* magazine with Eisenhower on the cover, a book on auction bridge by Ely Culbertson, and a dog-eared copy of *Lady Chatterley's Lover*. Thurber Farber had had eclectic taste in reading material.

I opened the door and peered in both directions down the shadowy hall. There was no sound from downstairs to indicate anyone had entered in the interim; the house seemed to be holding its breath, as was I. Resolutely reminding myself that I had to be in Joanie's car in ten minutes, I went to the top of the stairs, listened intently for a squeak or footstep, then went down and hurried to the kitchen.

In the first few cabinets, I found pots, pans, spices, and canned vegetables, but in the one next to the sink I found Maribeth's Ultima products: vitamins, packets of protein mixes (chicken soup, orange-flavored drink, and vanilla pudding, none of which sounded especially appetizing). I presumed the police had taken the bottles of potassium caplets. I glanced at my watch, then looked frantically around the kitchen, trying to think of a reason why Maribeth might have misplaced a bottle. My eyes landed on a bulging plastic garbage bag.

I bent over it and began digging through sour-smelling beer cans, whiskey bottles, coffee grinds, eggshells, greasy chicken bones, limp, oily lettuce, and all those delightful things one tends to discard over several weeks of riotous living. My fingers brushed a smooth plastic surface; I forced myself to plunge my hand all the way through the disgusting depths and grappled for it.

I came up with a plastic bottle. It had the Ultima label and through a patina of catsup and speckles of coffee grinds I could make out the word POTASSIUM. I shook it and was rewarded with the smallest rattle of what I dearly hoped was a solitary caplet. It was too late to dally in the kitchen for a round of self-congratulations. The bottle firmly in hand, I headed for the front door, debating whether to return the ladder to the shed or simply leave it there.

I unlocked the front door and opened it. Gerald Galleston stared at me, a key in one hand and a briefcase in the other. "What are you doing in my house?" he demanded harshly.

ELEVEN

I stuck my hand behind my back and forced a smile. "Oh, good, you're home early," I said, willing myself not to retreat down the hall. "I was hoping you'd get here before I had to leave, but now I'm afraid it's gotten late and I've got to pick up the girls at the fitness center. They're likely to be sweaty and exhausted, so I'd better run along."

He said exactly what I'd have said in the face of the above incoherent sputtering. "Huh?"

"The teen exercise class," I elaborated while assessing the amount of space on either side of him. "Bobbi makes them bop until they drop, or so Caron said. Or was it Jody? Now that I think about it, Bobbi may have told me that herself. In any case, I really must run along now."

Although he was not a large man, he managed to fill the doorway. Weaving just enough to keep both sides blocked, he said, "You still didn't explain why you're in my house. How'd you get in, anyway?"

"Didn't I explain all that? I . . . ah, came by to pick up a few things for Maribeth. A nightgown, maybe some cosmetics. In case she wakes up and wants to freshen up for her visitors. The door was open, but it was very naughty of me to come in like that, wasn't it?''

I tried a conspiratorial little laugh, but he wasn't in the mood. The more I studied him, however, the more I realized that he was weaving not to block any escape attempts but from a faulty balance mechanism, most likely produced by alcohol. His eyes were wandering in opposite directions; he kept blinking and squinting in an attempt to control them, but he was having little success.

"Door was locked," he said at last. "Whaddaya got behind your back, Claire?" He wrinkled his nose, then stepped back and snorted. "You stink worse than a month-old skunk carcass in the middle of the road. Holy Moses, I've been in slaughterhouses that smelled better than you do.''

I did not point out that any residual redolence was from his garbage, not mine. "I was in such a hurry I skipped my morning shower." I ostentatiously looked at my watch and gasped. "It's seven o'clock! I absolutely must leave, Gerald, so I'd deeply appreciate it if you'd let me by. Caron's beastly when she's kept waiting." I feinted to the left, then back to the right, but he somehow managed to anticipate my ladylike lunges and counter them.

"Why do you think I'd do something to Maribeth?" he demanded in a burst of belligerence. "I'm the last person to want her dead, damn it. She's getting more than ten million bucks in half a year. If she's not around to collect it, it goes to some fool charity or other, and I'll stay in genteel poverty the rest of my life. You think it's easy to live on what they pay at this pissant college? My father makes more than I do, and he works for a trucking company. A trucking company. Ha!''

"Perhaps your book will bring in a great deal of money.''

He sagged against one side of the doorway and let his head fall to the side, but he was watching me with a sly expression. "Real ironic, isn't it? You kick and fight and step on people and do everything possible to get above a blue-collar existence, but then you find out all it means is bigger bills and bigger headaches. Farther to fall. Take a wild guess what the hotshot candidate from Toledo just published.'' He grabbed my arm and shook it so violently I could hear the caplet rattle. His voice menacing, he said, ''Go on, take a goddamn guess.''

''Something on international trade regulations?''

''Says it's definitive. Says it got great reviews all over the damn place and already's been adopted at several major law schools.''

''What a pity,'' I murmured realizing I'd been coerced into backing most of the way down the hall. As I tried to decide how best to handle the unnerving situation, he took a step toward me, gave me a surprised look, and slowly crumpled to the floor.

I stepped over him, went back down the hall, conscientiously closed the door behind me, and fled to Joanie's car. If Gerald had been the least bit sober, I would have been obliged to come up with a halfway plausible explanation for being in his house. By the time he roused himself he might have forgotten the encounter, but I couldn't rely on that. The ladder was under the window, and there might be a muddy footprint or two in the upstairs bathroom. If Gerald called the police, it would result in a most uncomfortable confrontation, if not a felony warrant.

But I had the bottle tucked in my purse. As I pulled away from the curb, I saw the old woman and her filthy beast in the next yard, she feigning no awareness of what was happening to a neighbor's japonica. I waved. She stared. The dog continued its business.

I drove as quickly as I dared to the fitness center, trying to formulate an excuse that would mollify Caron. I was working on a story involving a runaway train as I pulled up in front of Delano's and parked. No one impatiently paced on the sidewalk. Assuming they were impatiently pacing inside, I opened the door and braced myself for a torrential outburst of music and acrimony.

The room was uninhabited, the offensive cassette player mute. Totally mystified, I sank down on the nearest chair and frowned at my reflection in the mirror on the opposite wall.

The day had not gone well. Peter had made my theory evaporate, at least temporarily. Someone had stolen my cotter pin in an effort to demobilize me in more ways than one. My bribee had betrayed me and was ten dollars richer for his effort. I could ignore the ticket I'd receive from campus security, but I couldn't ignore the mechanic's bill if I wanted my car back. Dr. Brandisi had not returned my call. Gerald had caught me in his house, and at that very moment might be whining to Peter about it. I smelled like a denizen of a landfill. I'd lost Caron and Inez.

All I had for my industriousness was a plastic bottle with one caplet in it. It was apt to be a potassium caplet, which meant I'd been pierced and bruised and banged up for absolutely nothing. Miss Marple-Malloy was a failure. A dismal failure. Not worthy of tea and crumpets, much less a gold medal for deductive prowess. Or silver. Not even bronze.

Bobbi came out of the office door, wearing a large white jacket over a leotard and carrying a canvas bag. She had a less than perky scowl on her face, but when she saw me, she almost leapt out of her leotard (white, with gold pinstripes to match her leg warmers). "What are you doing here?" she yelped.

"Resting, if you must know. I had an aerobic exercise of my own, although not to music by any means."

"Are you hurt?" she said, still eyeing me as if there were a fuzzy black spider spinning a web in my hair, an idea I did not care to entertain—nor to explore.

"Why would I be hurt?"

"I don't know. I mean, you said you were doing aerobics, and I thought you might have twisted your ankle or fallen or something."

"It wasn't quite that strenuous. Actually, I'm here to pick up Caron and Inez, but unless they're still in the dressing room, I'm too late."

"I always check the back rooms before I leave, and no one's here but me," she said firmly. "As for the girls, they waited around for a few minutes, then caught a ride with a friend. That was about ten or fifteen minutes ago." She gave me an odd look, as if anticipating a challenge. When I shrugged, she came across the room and sat down beside me. "Wow, we had some workout today. After I go to the hospital, I'm going home and just soak in the bathtub for hours and hours."

She was glowing from the earlier exertion, but she didn't look as though she needed to visit an emergency room. "The hospital?" I said blankly.

"Isn't it so exciting!"

"To be frank, I find them rather dreary. The antiseptic smell, the little rooms painted in revolting colors, the nurses recruited from penal colony staffs. I'm not sure I'd use the word 'exciting' to describe a hospital."

She sniffed several times, then made a face. "Ooh, the carpet smells terrible. Jody's got to fire the janitor; he obviously hasn't been doing his job. But I didn't mean the hospital was exciting, Mrs. Malloy. I think they're creepy, what with those big needles and bodily fluids and dead bodies in the basement. I was talking about Maribeth. I just thought you'd already heard."

"Has she come out of the coma?" I said, allowing the janitor to take the blame for the malodorous ambiance. When she nodded, I added, "This *is* exciting. When did it happen?"

"Gee, I don't know exactly. Jody's been calling the hospital every hour ever since the accident, and he told me right before the teen class that Maribeth had been moved to a private room. He was as excited as a little kid; he left early to take her some flowers."

At least he wouldn't have bumped into Gerald, unless some sort of resurrection had taken place without any celestial displays. "I think I'll run by for a visit too," I said. A nice little visit during which Maribeth could explain a few things. I stood up, started for the door, and then looked back at Bobbi. "Did you know that Maribeth's condition was caused by a potassium deficiency, that she didn't take any caplets for two weeks?"

Bobbi gave me a bewildered look. "I can't believe that.

One of the Ultima staff rules is to ask the client every single time if he or she is taking everything on the program. Maribeth always assured me that she was.''

''Was she upset when her steady weight loss dropped off and her progress slowed down?''

''The first time I was with her and she'd gained half a pound, she burst into tears, and I had an awful time calming her down. I was as distraught as she was. Then, a couple of visits later, when Candice was with another client, I weighed Maribeth, and she'd gained a little bit again. I was ready for her to start crying, but she just shrugged and didn't make a big deal about it. I told her it was probably just a temporary water gain, especially since every last bite on her food list for the three days before was legal. It was kind of funny, though, because afterward I wondered if Maribeth heard one word I said.''

''She was so spaced out those last few days that she might not have assimilated anything.''

''But she wouldn't lie to me about taking the potassium,'' Bobbi said, shocked. ''She was really friendly during the consultations. We just talked and talked about her husband and . . .'' She paused for a moment, twisting a curl around her finger and staring into the distance. ''You know, girl talk.''

''Hairstyles and boyfriends?''

Despite Caron's avowals to the contrary, Bobbi was capable of sweating, because I could see the beads forming on her forehead and upper lip. In an odd voice, she said, ''Clothes, hair, makeup, that kind of thing. One day she forgot her box of protein supplements and came back while Dr. Winder . . . Well, Shelly and I thought we were alone. I guess somebody might think it was a compromising position, although I just thought it was kind of funny. Maribeth's not the sort to tattle.''

''I wondered if you and Dr. Winder, ah, found each other attractive,'' I said, smiling in hopes of eliciting more girl talk. ''I hope you weren't too irritated with me the night I made him discuss Maribeth's chart while you were in the back room.''

"I wasn't," she said with a giggle, "but he was in a god-awful snit. His glasses fogged over and he stomped around for half an hour saying that you would blab all over town. For some reason, Shelly's real touchy about his reputation.''

"Did Maribeth say anything to you about Jody?''

"No.'' She stood up and fluffed her hair over her shoulders, her expression making it clear that giggly girlish confidences were done for the day. She wiggled her fingers at me, picked up her bag, and sailed out the door.

I sat for a moment, waiting for an intuitive flash. Nary a flicker came. I went to Joanie's car and drove toward the hospital, then turned at the last minute and headed for my apartment. I'd grown accustomed to my stench, but I doubted others would be quite so adaptable, particularly in those places where cleanliness ranked well above godliness.

I'd rehearsed an alibi for Caron, but she wasn't there. It was just as well, I thought, as I peeled off my shirt and stuffed it in the clothes hamper. I spent a good while in the shower. Telling lies required more mental dexterity than I possessed after being beaned with a brick, used as a dart board, and bounced off the roof of the car, all in less than seventy-two hours.

Amateur sleuthing has its drawbacks.

I dressed, combed my hair, and was at the door when the telephone rang. Presuming (or praying, anyway) that it was Dr. Brandisi, I opted to answer it with a cautious, "Hello?''

"Claire,'' Peter said with no perceptible warmth. "We need to talk. Can you come by the station?''

"I was on my way to the hospital,'' I said evenly. "Have you heard the good news about Maribeth Galleston?''

"The hospital's a couple of miles from your house, isn't it?''

"That's a fair estimate.''

"Quite a long walk, and even longer on the return, when it's dark.''

"It would be a long walk,'' I agreed.

"But not as far as to the Galleston house."

"It's probably twice as far," I agreed again, wishing I knew what he had on me. There were numerous possibilities.

"But not as far as the police station."

"No, the police station's quite a bit closer. Now that we've established the distances between my house and various local points of interest, I'd like to get to the hospital to visit Maribeth."

"Long walk."

"We've already done that one," I said acidly. "Twice as far to her house, but not as close as the police station. Contrary to certain disparaging opinions held of me, I can retain a certain amount of statistical data for at least sixty seconds. I'm sure you'll be relieved to learn I'm not planning to walk to any of those destinations."

"Shame about your car."

"This Gary Cooper imitation is getting tiresome. If you have something to say, say it in sentences complete with subjects and verbs. The only allowed exception is the short yet always popular 'good-bye.' "

"Oh, no, I'm not anywhere near ending this chat. It seems campus security called in a request to identify the owner of a particular license plate, in that the owner had committed the unspeakable sin of parking on the grass and then fleeing the scene of the crime. Jorgeson ran the license plate number, and guess whose name popped up like a clump of crabgrass?"

"I had a minor mechanical problem, but I hardly fled. I walked slowly to the administration building and called a tow truck. At the maintenance man's suggestion. He was concerned about the impending appearance of the mower."

"Jorgeson was bored, so he called the tow service to ascertain details. He was surprised to hear that the car in question had an unusual problem, not a minor mechanical one."

"Jorgeson has too much free time on his hands. Someone ought to reassign him to traffic control."

There was a long silence, long enough for me to realize the receiver was slippery from someone's sweaty grasp. Finally, when I was preparing to inquire if he was still there, I was treated to a lengthy sigh.

"Why didn't you call me as soon as this happened?" Peter said in a pained voice. "Or when the mechanic told you that someone had intentionally removed the cotter pin?"

"I didn't want to bother you in the middle of your big investigation. You know, Jockscam."

"You didn't want to bother me with the knowledge that someone tried to kill you? I'm deeply moved by this display of thoughtfulness on your part. Do you have any idea who was so unthoughtful as to remove the cotter pin and cause your brakes to fail?"

"The maintenance man had shifty eyes. He also took my ten dollars and called the damn security cops anyway. If that's not an indication of amorality, I don't know what is. Why don't you send idle Jorgeson over to fingerprint the grass?"

"I doubt he's up to that at the moment. Listen, Claire, when I told you about the test results, you promised to stop snooping around. Maribeth Galleston was involved in an unfortunate accident caused by her refusal to mention the childhood rheumatic fever and her failure to take the potassium caplets. That's all there is to it—no criminal intent, no conspiracy, no anything to make you start salivating over juicy clues. The district attorney said he doubts he'll bring any charges against her, although she'll have to live with the Winder woman's death for the rest of her life. I would imagine twelve million dollars will go a long way to assuage the guilt. No one, including her husband and her lover, had any reason to try to harm her with some crazy scheme involving pseudo-potassium caplets. Okay?"

"Then what happened to my cotter pin?"

"I don't know, but when I find him, I'll—" He broke off with a rather prehistoric growl. After a moment, he added, "I'll have someone check with your neighbors to see if anyone was seen skulking around your garage. In the meantime, lock the garage door, stop pestering people with your questions, and *stay away* from the Ultima Diet Center and Delano's Fitness Center.''

"All right, all right," I said meekly. "Am I allowed to visit Maribeth?''

"To visit, not to put her through the third degree. Jorgeson and I are going by tomorrow or the next day to find out what she has to say about the potassium, just to finalize the report. And one more thing, Claire . . . put things back where you find them. When the Gallestons can afford a gardener, he may need a ladder.''

It seemed prudent to mutter a good-bye and hang up, both of which I did while clutching the back of a chair. Once I'd recovered, I went downstairs and related the news to Joanie, who was eager to accompany me to the hospital. In that it was her car, I felt obliged to display some enthusiasm at the prospect. We went to the garage.

"Oh, my," Joanie said, fanning the air with her hand, "the car absolutely reeks. I know Caron and Inez are not fond of advice, but you have a maternal duty to discuss underarm deodorants and personal hygiene with them.''

Nodding, I rolled down the car window and watched the scenery while I tried to decide how best to grill Maribeth. By the time we arrived at the hospital, I'd failed to perfect a strategy and was prepared to improvise. As Joanie and I waited in front of the elevators, I spotted a familiar figure in a white coat.

The elevator door opened. I shoved Joanie in and said, "I'll catch up with you in a minute. I want to get Maribeth a little something from the gift shop.'' The door slid closed before she could protest, and I hurried down the corridor and caught Dr. Brandisi's arm. "Hello. I left a message earlier with your receptionist that I needed to speak to you.''

He gave me a wry smile. "I don't think she likes you. After you left, she wanted to report you to the Department of Human Services, but I talked her out of it. What did you need to speak to me about, Mrs. Malloy?''

"Maribeth had a potassium deficiency. I wondered if residual damage from rheumatic fever might have caused it, or had an effect on the severity of the symptoms.''

He shook his head. ''I'm not a specialist in dietary dysfunctions, but I don't see why there would be any correlation between the two. The rheumatic fever resulted in some damage to her heart. The potassium deficiency would make her forgetful, vague, sort of fluttery.''

''Or apt to fly into uncontrollable rages?''

''Rages?'' he repeated, giving me a puzzled look.

''One second she'd be smiling, the next in an absolute fury over an insignificant remark or question. It was almost a Jekyll-Hyde routine.''

''That sounds more like a roid rage,'' Brandisi said. He glanced at his watch, then gave me a sharp look and added, ''Do you have any reason to suspect she was taking anabolic steroids?''

''Steroids?'' I said incredulously. ''Why would she be taking steroids? They're not part of anyone's diet program, are they? How would she get them?''

''They're not hard to find these days. Locker rooms, playgrounds, bowling alleys—you name it. I've treated a couple of junior high boys who wanted to beef up their bodies without exerting themselves to do any more than gulp down pills. They were rather alarmed when they experienced testicular atrophy, rages, depression, acne, and were faced with the possibility of heart, liver, and kidney damage, not to mention permanent sterility. As for your friend, the steroids would have created serious complications because of the cardiovascular damage.''

I stared at him while I tried to assimilate the barrage of symptoms he'd tossed out so casually. ''Maribeth had developed acne,'' I said slowly, ''and was having an increasingly difficulty time losing weight.''

''Athletes use steroids to increase muscle mass. No one taking steroids will lose weight, although whether or not it actually enhances muscular strength and endurance is disputed in medical circles. Her physician surely knows about this, so you might talk to him. I've got to finish my rounds.''

"One more thing, Dr. Brandisi. I've got a caplet that's supposed to be potassium. Is it possible you could have the lab at the hospital run a test on it?"

His expression made it clear he was remembering his receptionist's dark opinions of my character. "You think it's a steroid? Is that why you want me to order the test?" He held up his hands and began to back away from me. "I'm afraid I can't help you, Mrs. Malloy. I didn't mind hunting up an old medical record, but I have no desire to get involved in something like this. You need to discuss this with a policeman, not a pediatrician. Now I really must finish my rounds; my wife's waiting in the lounge."

"One little caplet," I said, turning on the earnestness and moving toward him. "How long can it take to test one teeny tiny caplet? The hospital lab runs hundreds of tests every day; no one will mind one more minor test. The police have declined to become involved. The girl was a patient of your father's, and I'm sure he would want you to do whatever you can to help her."

"He might agree, but he didn't have to pay exorbitant malpractice premiums in case hysterical parents decide I should have diagnosed little Suzie's Ethiopian liver-worm disease when they forgot to mention the details of their vacation. I'm sorry, but I can't risk any involvement with another physician's case." With an apologetic shrug, he walked briskly down the corridor and vanished around the corner.

I went back to the elevators and punched a button, frantically trying to come up with a reason why Maribeth might have been taking steroids rather than potassium. I doubted she aspired to become a weight lifter, a lady wrestler, or a member of the Farber College Fighting Frogs. She certainly didn't want to increase her muscular bulk. It was time to ask her some hard questions.

The elevator door opened and I joined a green-clad orderly who was ogling a pair of shiny-faced nurses. I huddled in the corner until we reached Maribeth's floor, and then went down the hall to her room.

Maribeth was hooked up to tubes, and an oxygen tube was

taped across her nostrils. A broad strip of adhesive tape across her nose and cheeks and a misshapen purplish bruise on one side of her face attested to the force with which she'd hit the steering wheel. Her eyes were closed.

Joanie sat on the unoccupied bed. She gave me a pinched smile and said, "I'd about given up on you. Was there a crowd in the gift shop, or were you too busy chasing doctors down the hall to find it?"

"How's Maribeth?" I whispered. "Is she asleep?"

"She said she'd had several visitors in the last hour. They must have been too much for her."

Maribeth opened her eyes, and in a hoarse, nasal voice said, "Claire, how nice of you to come. I'm not a very good hostess, but sit down for a minute."

I sat on the arm of a chair, wishing I had the nerve to ask her some questions but aware of Joanie's protective presence. I settled for an innocuous, "How are you feeling, Maribeth?"

"Not good. I've got a broken nose, two cracked ribs, and enough needles stuck in me to make a pine tree. Then again, it's nice to be alive." She turned her head to one side, and swallowed several times. "Poor Candice. When I first woke up, the whole thing seemed like a nightmare, just a horrible fantasy someone had whispered in my ear while I was unconscious. Then this afternoon Jody showed up with flowers, and I made him tell me what happened. I almost killed you, too, Claire. You must be furious at me."

"No," I said sternly, "and you can't blame yourself for the accident. A freak accident, Maribeth. You can't hold yourself responsible for a heart attack that made you lose control of your car. It wasn't your fault."

"That's right," Joanie added.

"But it was my fault," Maribeth said. "I should have said something about my heart condition, but I didn't because I wanted to go on the Ultima program. I assumed they wouldn't take me if they thought I was a high-risk client."

"So you told them that you'd been examined by your personal physician?" I said, avoiding Joanie's dark look. "No one at the Ultima Center had any idea you'd had rheumatic fever as a child, and that there was a second occurrence in college?''

She stared at the ceiling for a moment, her eyes unblinking and her mouth slack. ''I didn't tell anyone at Ultima. Gerald might have mentioned it to Candice, I suppose, but nobody said anything to me about it.''

''And therefore you were allowed to stay on the program,'' I said with a sweetly inquisitive smile.

''Of course she stayed on the program,'' Joanie snapped. She crossed her legs and began to jiggle her foot up and down in an irritated way, as though she were visualizing making contact with someone's fanny. ''I think we'd better let Maribeth rest. Visitors can be tiring—and tiresome.''

''I did stay on the program,'' Maribeth continued. ''Bobbi came by earlier and asked me a lot of questions about those overly emotional outbursts. She implied that I'd skipped the potassium, but I took caplets three times a day. The only time I missed any was the day before I fainted in the Book Depot, and that scared me.''

''The police found three full bottles at your house,'' I said.

''Gerald brought me some, didn't he?'' she said, sounding confused. ''I thought it was just one bottle, but maybe he had others. That's the only explanation that makes sense.'' She put her hand on her forehead, then let it slide down her cheek, tracing the border of the bruise. ''Aren't Jody's flowers beautiful?''

Joanie clucked admiringly. ''They're quite beautiful.''

I made a similar noise, then said, ''He's been terribly worried about you. Bobbi said earlier that he's been calling the hospital every hour since the accident.''

''He told me,'' she said in an amazed voice. ''He said he's been skipping lunch because he misses our little picnics in the office.'' She gave me a secretive smile that seemed to imply complicity between the two of us, although one of us was decidedly on the far side of the moon. ''I don't know what I'd do if something happened to Jody. You understand, don't you? We're pretty much still in the same boat.''

I'd heard it before, but I had yet to figure out if the boat to which she kept referring was the *Andrea Doria* or the *QEII*. I resorted to inanity. "Certainly."

"The same boat," she repeated. "Joanie may not understand, but we do. Right, Claire?"

"Right," I said with admirable conviction.

Suddenly tears began to spill down Maribeth's cheeks, and her voice grew so painfully hoarse that I could barely understand her. "You know what I was? I was a weapon. It was as though someone had loaded me with a bullet and pointed me at Candice's heart. I never would have hurt her. I didn't even care that she and Gerald were—you know."

"You must rest now," Joanie said abruptly. "Our visit has upset you, and I'm sure you're exhausted. Come along, Claire."

We murmured good-byes and left the room. As we approached the elevator, Joanie said, "There you are. She was taking the caplets regularly. Either someone at Ultima was giving her placebos, or her rotten husband was switching them."

"Placebos or something a bit stronger. The doctor I spoke to in the lobby said her symptoms sounded like they might be the result of anabolic steroids."

"That's absurd."

"I agree, and we still don't have a solid motive."

"You haven't discovered it."

I acknowledged the veracity of her accusation with a sigh. My purse thudded against my hip, and I heard, or imagined I heard, the rattle of a lone caplet. I realized I couldn't tell Joanie about it, because she would demand to know how it came to be in my possession. Those of us without transportation needed to tread very carefully, if we didn't want to trudge home in the dark. "Okay, we'll presume she took the caplets as prescribed by the Ultima staff. Candice, Sheldon, and Bobbi were the only ones who could have made the substitution at the center. Gerald could have done so at home. But she lied when she said she was losing steadily."

"Not Maribeth Farber Galleston," Joanie said, punching

the elevator button so hard I could almost hear a minute electronic squeal of agony. We drove home in an uneasy silence, and I was relieved when I could say good night and go upstairs. I was not relieved when I discovered Caron was not home. I checked her bedroom, which was in its usual state of artful chaos, and found no indication she'd been there in my absence. Bobbi had told me Caron and Inez had waited for me, then accepted a ride with a friend. What friend?

I called Inez's house, but no one answered and I remembered Inez had mentioned that her parents would be at a meeting. The girls could have gone to the college library, one of their favorite places to analyze male behavior in a relatively safe (no one ever noticed them) environment, but Caron would have eaten spiders before setting foot outside in the ragged gym shorts and T-shirt she'd been wearing.

And they didn't know anyone in the aerobics class, except Bobbi, who was still there when I arrived and therefore hadn't given them a ride. Jody had gone to the hospital to visit Maribeth. I found the telephone directory, looked up Bobbi's number, and dialed it. No one answered.

My fingers felt numb as I found the number of Delano's Fitness Center. I let it ring half a dozen times, and was about to give up when a male voice answered with an impatient "Yes?"

"This is Claire Malloy," I said. "Is Bobbi Rodriquez there?"

"Hey, this is Jody, Claire. Bobbi's not here. Is there something I can help you with?"

"I don't think so. I was half an hour late to pick up Caron and Inez, and Bobbi said they'd accepted a ride from a friend. That was almost two hours ago, and they haven't come home. I wanted to ask Bobbi who offered the ride." I tried to laugh, but it came out a shade too high. "I'm sure everything's fine. Mothers do worry, though."

"I should say so. My mama used to whack me if I was one minute late for supper. Bobbi said she had some kinda appointment tonight, but she didn't say where she would be.

I know what I can do. There are only half a dozen girls in that class; how about I call them and see if any of them gave your daughter and her friend a ride someplace?''

"That would be great," I said. He promised to call me back, and after I hung up, I poured myself a shot of scotch and waited on the sofa, determined not to allow myself to entertain ghastly thoughts of perverts, kidnappers, or misogynists. I told myself over and over that at that very minute one of the girls in the class was telling Jody she'd dropped Caron and Inez at a movie theater—or, more likely, a pizza joint or the ice cream parlor on Thurber Street. Perhaps they'd stopped by Inez's house and Caron had borrowed more presentable clothes for the evening. Caron had been too irritated by my tardiness to bother to call or come by to leave a note.

The telephone rang. I grabbed it and said, "Yes?"

"I found out something," Jody said in a strained voice. "One of the girls, Bettina, said the two left with a man, an older guy who was working out on the machines in the back room. I wasn't here, so I didn't see him, and Bettina had never seen him before. I keep those records in a separate file, so if you want, you can come look through the file and see if you recognize any names."

"Bettina didn't describe the man?"

"Nah, she said she just noticed them leaving and didn't think anything about it until I called her. There's not more than a hundred names. You'll recognize one of them, call from here, and he'll say that he took the girls to the movie theater or whatever. If that doesn't work, Bobbi's car is parked out back, so she must have hitched a ride earlier. She'll hafta come back to pick it up."

I agreed, but after I'd hung up, I remembered that my car was in the shop. Damn. I put on a jacket, grabbed my purse, and went downstairs to knock on Joanie's door and further my career as a world-class liar.

She came to the door in a bathrobe, her gray hair wound tightly around spongy pink catepillars. "Yes?"

"I need to borrow your car."

"It's nearly ten o'clock, Claire. Wherever are you going at this hour?"

I couldn't admit I'd lost Caron and Inez because I had been delayed in Gerald's foyer. "Caron left something at the fitness center. Her math book."

"I certainly don't want to live below a math failure, so I'll get the car key for you. Something occurred to me while I was eating dinner, and it's been bothering me ever since. If the doctor Betty Lou overheard in intensive care did numerous tests on Maribeth, wouldn't he have informed Peter that there were steroids in her system?"

I was too worried about Caron and Inez to do more than shrug, but as I drove toward Delanon's Fitness Center her question echoed over and over again.

TWELVE

The front room of the fitness center was gloomy, but I could see a sliver of light under the office door. Feeling like a feverish woodpecker, I rapped on the glass with the car key until the office door opened and Jody crossed the room to admit me.

"Guess you haven't heard from them?" he asked as we went to the office. "Kids these days don't think about their parents, don't think anyone worries when they stay out late. Here's the membership forms on all the guys what use the back room. Most of them are bodybuilders, but we get some yuppie types, men and women both, who're trying to fight off middle age."

I wasn't capable of conversation, so I sat down behind the desk and began to thumb through the forms, some yellowed with age and others so fresh the ink might be wet. The names seemed relentlessly unfamiliar, but I'd never desired to meet people who want their bodies to bulge in unnatural ways and glisten as though they'd bathed in sunflower oil. I was nurturing some unnatural thoughts when I spotted a name I recognized.

"This one," I said, flapping the form. "He's a professor

in the English department. I don't know if Caron's seen him in five years, but he might remember her.''

Jody took the form and squinted at it. "Naw, look here where I record the monthly charges. He hasn't been an active member in six months.''

I deflated back into the chair and resumed my search. The names were in no particular order, and they began to blur as I battled with a panicky urge to sling them down and burst into tears. Ridgway. Nehr. Hart. Montgomery. Mertz. Baxter. Jorgeson. Adamson. Harrington . . .

Jorgeson.

I dropped the forms in my hand and very carefully went back through the ones I'd discarded until I found Jorgeson. As in Sergeant Jorgeson. As in Peter's minion. I licked my lips until I felt able to speak, then said, "May I please use your telephone?''

"Did you find the guy?''

"I believe so.'' With admirable control, I called the station and asked to speak to Peter Rosen. When he came on the line, I maintained the same level of control and merely inquired if he had seen Caron and Inez.

"They ought to be home by now. They talked Jorgeson into going out for hamburgers, but that was more than an hour ago.''

"Did Jorgeson consider the possibility that I might be wondering where they've been for the last three hours, that I might be entertaining thoughts of seedy men in raincoats with pockets full of candy?''

There was a long silence. "I'm afraid it's my fault. Jorgeson brought them to the station right after you and I had our chat. I was under the impression you were coming here, so I let them fool around my office until I could no longer bear it, then slipped Jorgeson ten bucks to take them away. I'm really sorry if you were worried about them.''

"I was worried,'' I admitted, sighing. I put my hand over the receiver and said to Jody, "They're both safe at home.''

"Thank God,'' he said. He cocked his head. "I think I heard something in one of the back rooms. The way the plumbing is these days, it could be a busted pipe. I'd better check it out."

I waited until he left, then removed my hand and said, "Just what was Jorgeson doing at a fitness center?"

"Getting in shape for the annual physical exam. I could use some exercise myself, although I'd rather wrestle something soft and warm than a cold, heartless barbell. Meet me at my apartment?"

"You lied to me earlier today," I said.

"I did? Then you must allow me to make it up to you in some way. How about a bottle of burgundy and the first fire of the season?"

"Well, it was more of an omission," I said, lecturing myself not to be distracted by the image of wine and the cozy sofa in front of the fireplace. "Of course you forgot to have Caron call me from the station, so perhaps you also forgot to mention that Maribeth had steroids in her system."

"Where'd you hear that?" he said quickly.

I leaned back in the chair and propped my feet on Jody's desk. Permitting an edge of modest triumph in my voice, I said, "Oh, here or there. I hear so many interesting things these days that I muddle my sources. Maribeth wasn't taking them on purpose; she thought she was taking potassium. Someone made the substitution without her knowledge, which means it had to be one of the Ultima staff or her husband. Did anyone fingerprint the bottles found in her kitchen?"

He began to rumble at me, but I was too busy staring at my purse to listen to him. A muffled thud from somewhere in the fitness center jarred me out of the trance.

"I'll call you when I get home," I said into the receiver and replaced it soundlessly. I eased the chair back and crept across the office to the doorway. "Jody?" I called softly.

There was no response. Light coming through the front window lay in angular paths across the carpet, and the plastic plants were silhouettes of ludicrous insects frozen in time and space. My feet were merely frozen.

"Jody?" I repeated, forcing myself to move out of the

perceived protection of the office. Something moved against the wall. I toyed with the idea of a heart attack until I realized it was my reflection in the mirror. I made it across the room and went down the short hallway lined with doors that led to the dressing rooms, sauna, and Jacuzzi. It had been several weeks since I'd attended the aerobics class with Maribeth, and I wasn't sure which door was which.

I told myself it was not the classic lady-tiger dilemma, nor was I apt to intrude on someone stepping out of his jockey shorts. However, I couldn't bring myself to open any of the doors, and had decided to return to the office and call Peter for assistance when the door behind me banged open and Jody stumbled forward. I grabbed his arm to prevent him from crashing into the concrete-block wall and hung on to him until he regained his balance.

"Claire?" he grunted, rubbing his head. "You okay?"

"I'm in better shape than you. What happened?"

"I don't know. I was checking the rooms, and all of a sudden something comes down on the back of my head. Help me to the office, will you? My knees ain't working too well."

"I think we'd better get out of here," I whispered, slipping my arm around him to steady him. "We can drive to the nearest pay phone and call the police."

"Yeah, I don't know what I'm saying. Lemme get the cash receipts out of the office and we'll split like bananas, okay?"

It wasn't exactly what I had in mind, but he was heading for the office and I was afraid to remove my arm. Looking over my shoulder with every step, I managed to get him to the office and close the door behind us. Once I'd helped him to the chair behind the desk, I said, "Did someone hit you?"

His face was pale and his breathing loud and uneven. He cautiously explored his head, then looked at his hand and said, "No blood. Blood scares me like I was a girl. No offense meant. You were real cool and collected back there. Thanks for keeping me from flattening my nose on the wall."

"You're welcome," I said nervously, wishing the office door had a nice, sturdy look. "If you'll get the receipts, we really ought to leave the building and call the police."

He groaned. "I don't know if I can make it to the car. I'm seeing stars, and we're not exactly in a planetarium. Let me get hold of myself for a minute; it won't do us any good if you have to drag me all the way to the door."

"Call them from here," I ordered.

He blinked at the telephone, then picked up the receiver and held it to his ear. "Nothing. Line's dead."

"Then it's been cut," I said grimly. "I'll help you out to the car, Jody. You don't have a plumbing problem; you've got a prowler who doesn't object to using force. Are you sure you didn't catch a glimpse of anyone?"

"You know what?" he muttered, screwing up his face so that he resembled a Pekingese. "I could almost swear I smelled something, something sweet like flowers. Does that make sense?"

"If it was perfume . . . Is there any way Bobbi could have returned without your knowledge?"

"I was in here with the door shut, calling those girls and waiting for you. If she was real quiet, she could unlock the front door, creep across the front room, and hide out in the ladies dressing room, and I might not have heard her. But why would she want to do something stupid like that? All she had to do was tell me she was here."

"I suggest the police take up the question," I said, watching the door. "The receipts, my purse, and we are out of here." I opened my purse to find Joanie's car key, then looked up at the sound of his sudden inhalation.

Jody stared at the potassium bottle. "Why's that in your purse?"

"I took it from Maribeth's garbage this afternoon. Shall we go?"

He continued to stare at the bottle, and I could tell from his wrinkled forehead that he was doing his best to think. A delay of that magnitude was inopportune, so I said, "I'm not sure what's going on, but Bobbi may have substituted steroids for the potassium in order to cause Maribeth's heart attack."

"Why?" Jody said, his eyes riveted on the bottle.

"Let's talk about it in the car, shall we?" I found the car

key and held it up, noting that my hand was trembling like a cloud of gnats.

"Why would Bobbi do that to Maribeth?"

"How should I know? Maybe she thought she could blame it on Candice and end up with Sheldon," I said irritably.

He sat back down, which did nothing to encourage me, and in a stunned voice, said, "That's not why she did it, Claire. Have you noticed that jerk she hangs around with— the kid with the red car who's all the time scowling like he needs to pee and knows it's going to sting? His name's Marcus."

"He was here the first time I came, and was parked outside a few nights ago. We haven't been formally introduced."

"He's her boyfriend, and he's a real loser. He used to bug me about getting him steroids and corticosteroids and all those illegal drugs. He wanted enough to supply the entire athletic department. I finally kicked him out and told him he couldn't even show up at the center, much less work out, but I know Bobbi was seeing him after work almost every day. What if he put the screws on her, and she sweet-talked Winder into helping her get the drugs to pass along to him? Winder's in shaky financial shape; he probably wouldn't mind a little cash flow on the side."

Ninety percent of me was eager to leave, but the remainder was entranced by Jody's narrative. The minority ruled. "But why would she give Maribeth steroids?"

"Maybe Maribeth saw something, some transaction between them after her aerobics class." He banged his fist on the desk. "It makes my blood boil to think about Bobbi doing that to Maribeth. It came damn close to killing her, especially since Maribeth had that heart problem from when she was a kid."

"Some of your theory works," I said slowly, "but how did Bobbi get into the Gallestons' house to replace the steroids with innocent potassium? Gerald keeps the house locked. If we add him to the group, we're up to four conspirators."

"That wimp? He couldn't conspire to piss in a pot. Bobbi

must have taken Maribeth's key from her purse and had a copy made of it. The cops'll find it."

"Speaking of which, we need to get out of here," I said, having finally remembered the wisdom of a timely exit. Bobbi was petite, but she was in excellent condition from countless aerobics classes. Her brutish boyfriend was not someone I wanted to encounter in a dark alley—or a dark dressing room.

"I'm not going to let anyone chase me out of my own place of business," Jody said as he bent down to open a drawer. When he sat up. he had a small yet unpleasant gun in his hand, and a decidedly unpleasant expression on his face. "Not Bobbi, not Marcus, not anybody in the whole damn world. You go call the police. I'm going to see if someone's still hanging around."

"That's crazy, Jody. You don't know how many people are out there, or whether they've got guns too. You've got to leave with me."

"After what they did to Maribeth, they're going to answer to me, Joseph Delano. Now you go call the cops; I can take care of myself."

I picked up my purse and moved hesitantly toward the door. "I don't like this. We're not at the O.K. Corral and it's long past noon. You're not in any shape to skulk around in the dark, playing some macabre game with a party or parties unknown."

He rose and crossed the room, took me by the shoulder, and shoved me out into the main room. "Go call the cops," he said in an insistent whisper. "The quicker you call, the quicker they'll get here."

It was the first sensible thing he'd said. "All right," I said crossly, then watched him melt through the door that led to the workout machines. In lieu of a bulletproof vest, I clutched my purse to my chest and waited for a sound, any sound, that would give me an idea of what was happening. Jody was dazed from the blow to his head. It seemed as if it might have been Bobbi who had attacked him, but only because he'd thought he smelled something sweet, and olfactory flashes are not dependable when one is bashed. And what could have provoked her into the attack?

I'd mentioned the potassium deficiency several hours earlier, and Bobbi had said she was planning to go by the hospital. If she'd hitched a ride, she would need to return for her car. But why come inside the fitness center and creep around in the dark, then hide in a dressing room and bash Jody? It seemed more practical to pick up her car, drive home, pack a bag, and leave town.

It seemed equally practical for me to leave the building, find a telephone, and send in the cavalry, but I continued to hesitate by the door, straining to hear a voice or a footstep. I had not been in the back room, so I had no idea how large it was, or if it had doors to the dressing rooms, et al.

Something wafted across the doorway, but so quickly I wasn't sure I hadn't worked myself into such a nervous dither that I'd seen the Phantom of the Weight Room. I decided to take a quick look for Jody to warn him; if I couldn't find him, I would get myself out of there as quickly as possible. I went to the doorway. There was less light and no sense of movement. The machines were glinting metallic skeletons, some tall, some squat, and all contorted and bizarre. A graveyard of dinosaurs.

"Jody?" I whispered. Recklessness overrode terror, and I edged into the room and whispered his name again. I moved around what I deemed to be a Pectoralsaurus, avoided a Tricepstopis, and crept to the door I saw in one corner. As I eased it open, I heard a loud explosion. A gunshot.

Terror overrode recklessness, and I backpaddled into a machine that ripped at my leg, then turned and blundered into a second that caught me just above the knees and sent me head first onto the floor. My purse flew out of my hands and the contents scattered into the darkness. I opened my eyes in time to see the potassium bottle roll under a machine and disappear.

It was the only evidence that linked the Ultima Center with the scheme to kill Maribeth. I got to my knees and crawled in the direction the bottle had rolled. It was not lodged under the bench contraption. I continued on my mad hunt, aware that someone had fired a gun in the building. Had Jody shot Bobbi? Had Bobbi shot Jody? Had Bobbi's boyfriend shot one of them, and did he still have a bullet or two to spare?

A fluorescent light came on overhead, brutally bright. I scrunched under the bench, trying my best to be invisible, but two feet came across the room and stopped a few inches from my nose.

"Claire? I thought you went to call the police?"

"Jody," I said with a whoosh of relief, "thank God you're all right." I rolled out from under the machine and stood up. "I heard a shot fired, and I was afraid you'd been hurt. What happened?"

He rubbed his face with his hands, his shoulders hunched as if we were in a blizzard rather than a room filled with equipment that looked strange even in the light. "Bobbi was in the storage room all the way at the back, stuffing bottles and packages in her bag. I guess that's where she was keeping the drugs. Anyway, I showed her the gun and told her we were going to the office to wait for the police. Halfway down the hall, she jumped me. It was my fault, but I was having a hard time with her being a drug pusher and using my center. She's been doing an aerobics class or two for a couple of years."

He sat down on a particularly torturous-looking machine and stared numbly at the floor. I sat down beside him and touched his arm. "Then what happened?" I said.

"She's pretty strong for a girl—no offense intended. She grabbed my wrist, and I tried to jerk free, and we both crashed through the door into the Jacuzzi room. The gun just kind of went off of its own accord." He broke off and took a deep breath, then said in a low voice, " She took it in the gut. She gave me this godawful look, then fell back. I grew up in the Bronx and I've seen enough street fights to know there wasn't anything I could do for her, so I was heading for the front door when I heard a noise in here." He gave me a perplexed look, as if he'd just realized my presence. "I thought you went to call the police, Claire. It seems like forever, but it must have been five or ten minutes ago.''

"I was too worried about you, but I think I'd better call them now.'' My knees were as sturdy as tomato aspic, but I managed to stand up and gather the contents of my purse, including the pesky potassium bottle that had rolled all the way to the wall. I followed Jody into the main room.

The window was ablaze with blinking blue lights and the glare of flashlights shining in our faces. More blue lights were speeding through the parking lot, and shadowy figures darted in front of the window like commandos on a midnight maneuver. A fist pounded on the door, and an imperious voice shouted, "Open up! Police!''

Jody opened the door to admit several uniformed officers, and one grim lieutenant in a three-piece suit. Jorgeson followed his boss. When he saw me, gave me an apologetic smile.

The lieutenant was less cordial. "Are you all right?'' he snapped at me, looking as if he wanted to grab me by the arms and shake me with the fury of a bulldog (which I presumed he did).

"I'm fine. Bobbi Rodriquez, on the contrary, is not. She attacked Jody, and they got into a struggle over his gun,'' I said. "Down that way, in one of the back rooms.''

"She had hold of my wrist,'' Jody said miserably. "I can't believe it. She was a nice kid, a little bouncy at times, but a nice, clean kid—until she met that football jerk. She's in that first room on the left.''

Peter gazed stonily at me, then stalked down the hall, pushed open the door, and flipped on the light. I'd trailed silently after him, but I let out a gasp as I looked over his shoulder.

Bobbi floated facedown in the Jacuzzi, her arms spread as if she were lazily observing marine life through a mask. The Jacuzzi was on, sending streams of bubbles from each side and making small waves that made Bobbi's body drift lazily. But a ribbon of blood curled from under her, then dissipated

THIRTEEN

Shortly thereafter the hallway and Jacuzzi room were swarming with the investigative team, and Jody and I were escorted to the office to wait until Lieutenant Rosen had time for us. A uniformed cop watched us from beside the door, his hand resting on his weapon and his expression icy.

It was approaching midnight by now. I hadn't left a note when I dashed to Delano's to find a clue to Caron's whereabouts; now she was at home and probably worried about me. I picked up the receiver and was rewarded with a dial tone. I called my house and braced myself for an onslaught of accusations.

"Hello," Caron said in a thick voice.

"Hello, dear, I'm glad you made it home safely."

"Yeah, well, Jorgeson gave us a ride."

"So I learned after worrying about you for four hours," I said, frowning at the telephone. "Didn't you think about letting me know where you were all that time?"

"I didn't know where *you* were all that time. You're the one who forgot to pick us up. Anyway, can I go back to sleep now? I'm sort of tired from the aerobics class." She loosed a yawn of epic proportion to melodramatize her point.

"Wait a minute," I said. "Don't you want to know where I am?"

"Not especially, but if you insist, I'll write down the number on something. Hold on till I find a pencil."

I waited until she announced she'd found one, then told her I was at Delano's Fitness Center and apt to be there for several more hours. This seemed to wake her up, and she demanded to know what was going on. I explained as best I could.

"This is totally terrible," Caron said. "I just saw Bobbi a few hours ago. She can't be dead. Not someone like her. She doesn't even sweat—she glows. Or glowed, anyway."

"It was an accident," I said, steeling myself not to think of the corpse in the champagne bath. I glanced at the guard, then lowered my voice. "Did she seem normal when you and Inez left with Jorgeson?"

She thought for a minute. "Yeah, I guess so. The class was normal, which means we carried on like hyperactive pom-pom girls for an hour. Afterwards, Inez and I waited forever by the door"—a hint of accusal crept into her voice—"and Bobbi came over and asked us if we needed a ride. Then Jorgeson came out from the back room, so I asked him if Peter had finally carried out his threats to arrest you, and Jorgeson laughed in a squirmy way and said he'd give us a ride to the police station so we could look in all the cells. Bobbi asked if we were coming to any more classes. I said I didn't know and we left. That's about it."

"So she knew Jorgeson was a police officer?"

"I suppose so." There was a moment of silence. "Uh, I've sort of got a date this weekend," she added uncomfortably.

"You do? That's . . . wonderful. Who's the lucky guy?"

"Louis Wilderberry. He called to apologize for making that dumb remark to Rhonda Maguire. He said she had it all wrong and was just being bitchy when she repeated it to Inez. He also said that Rhonda's thighs jiggle like Jello when she walks, and that she ought to be arrested the next time she wears a miniskirt."

"And you're giving up the diets?"

"Of course not. First thing in the morning Inez and I are starting this diet where you eat six little meals a day instead of three, but you have to—"

I told her to go back to sleep and that I'd see her in the morning. As I hung up the telephone, Peter and Jorgeson came into the office. Peter had a canvas bag in his hand. He unzipped it and dumped the contents on the desk.

"Is this what Bobbi was putting in her bag when you found her in the storage room?" he asked, looking at Jody.

There were at least a dozen bottles and twice that many cylindrical amber pill containers. A plastic bag held several small glass bottles with rubber across their tops. A package of disposable syringes glinted evilly. Very pharmaceutical for an innocuous canvas bag.

Jody nodded. "I saw her scooping things into her bag. It looked like that stuff."

Jorgeson picked up a pencil and moved the plastic bag aside. "And look at that, Lieutenant," he said with a whistle. "A shiny key with hardly any scratches. Must have been made not too long ago."

Having been studiously ignored by all, I was fairly certain I was invisible, but I decided to find out if I was also inaudible. I went around the desk to study the illicit substances. "The key to the Gallestons' house? By the time you bothered to test the potassium caplets, Bobbi had already been there to make the switch."

Peter looked through me at Jorgeson. "I wonder if this might be a key to the Gallestons' front door. Have all of this fingerprinted, and send one of the uniformed officers to the house to see if the key works. Also, take a photograph of Rodriquez and run it by the places in town that make keys. Maybe someone will remember her."

"Excuse me," I said, "but—"

Peter flashed his teeth at me, but the dear little laugh lines around his eyes did not deepen. "Mrs. Malloy may want to mention that if the key does not work, the ladder is conveniently situated under an upstairs window. However, in that we are sworn to uphold the law, we'll just use the front door. With the owner's permission. Mrs. Malloy is unfamiliar with the approach.''

"I have a potassium bottle from the house," I said. "I found it in the bottom of the garbage bag. It's filthy, but it may have prints on it. Mine, Maribeth's, and Bobbi's, for instance."

Peter crossed his arms and gave me a mildly quizzical look. "You broke into the house, carried away evidence, and failed to tell me about it? Do I have this right?"

At least I wasn't invisible anymore, in that Peter, Jody, Jorgeson, and the guard were all staring at me as if I'd claimed to be Hitler in drag. I cleared my throat and said, "That's an oversimplification of facts, but you have the gist of it. I was going to hand over the bottle as soon as I found out if it was relevant. It's only been in my purse since seven o'clock."

Peter held out his hand. I sat down and opened my purse, took out the stained bottle, and passed it over with a little sniff. He scowled at it, then put it down and said, "Anything else in your purse you'd like to share with us? A smoking gun? A basketball ticket? A junior G-man badge?"

"No." I closed my purse. The resultant click reminded me of an earlier thought, and I tried to recall why my purse seemed significant. It had had a hard day, along with the rest of us. Thrown about in my car, squeezed under the seat of Joanie's car, bloated with the potassium bottle, abandoned on the desk when we'd heard Bobbi in the back room, and clutched to my chest when I'd gone to warn Jody. Busy, busy.

I examined it for signs of ravage. Unlike its owner, who was scarred and sore, it was unscathed. In deference to its loyalty in sticking with me through all the gruesomeness, I decided to give it a vacation on the top shelf of my closet.

Then it hit me, and I said to no one in particular, "It's odd that Bobbi had a copy of Maribeth's key. When did she have it made? Bobbi couldn't have taken the key during a consultation at Ultima. Maribeth didn't leave her purse in the reception room; she took it with her. She did leave it in the dressing room during the aerobics class, and also when she worked out on the weight machines. But Bobbi was occupied next door until six o'clock, so she couldn't have slipped into the dressing room, snitched the key, and returned it later.''

''Somebody else was snooping in the back?'' Jody laughed nervously. ''I'm going to have to beef up security around this place. You think Marcus was in the ladies' dressing room, pawing through purses?''

''You threw him out several weeks ago. He's not a gossamer sort who can flit around unnoticed during an aerobics class. He didn't even have the nerve to park out in front. The other night when you came out for a cigarette, he was parked way at the end of the row, by the dental clinic.''

Jody rubbed the back of his head. ''This is creepy,'' he said to Peter. ''I hope you guys get him quick. In the meantime, how about you put a guard in Maribeth's hospital room? I don't want him getting to her.''

''I think she's safe,'' I said, still talking aloud to myself. ''There's something else that puzzles me, though. She admitted she kept the rheumatic fever a secret from the Ultima staff, which meant she had to lie on the medical history form. We all thought she lied about the potassium, but she didn't: she was taking caplets faithfully. The problem is that they were steroids, but that wasn't her fault. After a while, they caused her to gain weight, and again we assumed she was lying when she claimed she was steadily losing.''

''She was real ashamed about it,'' Jody said. ''I felt bad for her, but all I could do was keep encouraging her.''

Peter was watching me, and a few layers of frost had melted. ''But what if Mrs. Malloy is correct and Maribeth wasn't lying? There had to be some reason she could ignore the scales at the Ultima Diet Center. Someone had to have convinced her that those scales were wrong, and another set was more accurate.''

''Caron Malloy lost three pounds in an hour,'' I said, nodding. ''Inez lost three, too. Maribeth was off by three pounds; she claimed to have lost seventeen pounds, but the Ultima record indicated fourteen. Quite a coincidence, isn't it? I didn't ask the girls where they'd made the discovery, but

I think they may have weighed themselves here. Shall I call and ask?"

"That rusty piece of junk in the weight room?" Jody said, his lip curled. "I just keep it to impress the yuppies with how fully equipped the gym is. Trust me, nobody in her right mind would think it's better than the shiny new ones next door."

I blinked at him. "But not one of them *was* in her right mind. One had not only a severe potassium deficiency that caused her to be flighty and forgetful, but also enough steroids in her system to keep her in a highly agitated state. As for the other two, they're fifteen years old and therefore are controlled solely by hormones and phases of the moon."

"Maybe the scales are off," Jody muttered.

"But Maribeth trusted them, perhaps with encouragement to do so. She's a very trusting person, isn't she? Vulnerable because of her weight problem, and as eager as a puppy to trust people who profess to cherish her despite it. She was desperate for attention, for any display of kindness—such as steamy kisses or long-stemmed roses. When someone wrote a message asking her to trust him, she did. She went so far as to imply it was from her husband, who wanted her to trust him while he busily committed her to a psychiatric ward so he could enjoy her money at his leisure."

"Her husband hadn't even been by to visit when I was there," Jody said, his lip curling higher to expose stained teeth.

"He's incapacitated at the moment," I said. Peter twitched, but I ignored it and continued. "Maribeth was so trusting that she was willing to believe a cockeyed story about an undercover cop and try to include me in the secret. She kept insisting she and I were in the same boat, but I didn't make the connection. She mentioned it minutes before her accident and again in her hospital room."

Jody lit a cigarette and leaned back in his chair. "Yeah, but it's a leaky rowboat and you're using one oar."

"I don't think so," I said. "Maribeth believed the undercover story, and she also believed the scales here were more accurate than the ones at the Ultima Center. She might have become suspicious if she dieted diligently yet began to gain weight. She might have examined the vitamins and supplements more carefully, and realized someone had made a substitution, perhaps someone who knew about her heart condition and was aware how steroids would aggravate it. When she told you she'd gained weight, you reset the scales here and convinced her yours were correct."

"You're crazier than a crack addict," Jody said. "Tell me how I asked her real nicely to give me a house key so I could sneak into her house."

"She wasn't that feather-brained. I've already explained a woman doesn't leave her purse lying around just anywhere, but she does have to set it down to pedal a stationary bicycle or leap around the room to music. If she'd been next door at the Ultima Center for a consultation first, at least once a week she'd have a plastic bag of vitamins, protein supplements, and potassium caplets with her. It's rather logical to assume she'd leave the bag beside her purse."

Jody turned to Peter and made a face. "This girl friend of yours is something, isn't she? No offense, but she's got a wild imagination. She ought to be selling her stories to some Hollywood producer in a leisure suit and sunglasses. I hope you're not buying this, Lieutenant."

"As odd as she is," said lieutenant said, "she often meddles with uncanny accuracy. While Maribeth was occupied in the sauna after the class, you could have switched the potassium caplets for steroids. While she was pedaling, you could have borrowed the house key and had a copy made so that you could make the exchange should the necessity arise."

"I could have been a contender, too, but that doesn't make it true," he retorted angrily. "I love Maribeth. When she divorces that husband of hers, I'm going to ask her to marry me so I can take care of her and make sure she maintains her goal. Why would I do all that dumb stuff to hurt her?"

Peter raised his eyebrows at me. "Mrs. Malloy?"

"Well," I murmured, "let's presume for a moment that Bobbi and her dear Shelly weren't involved in the sale of steroids to local athletes. Instead, let's presume that Jody didn't refuse to deal with the distasteful Marcus. After the football player died, it seemed prudent to avoid any association. That left the problem of transporting the illegal substances from here to the campus. Maribeth was absolutely delighted to run little errands for you, and no one could have ever imagined her in the role of dope runner. When did she first become suspicious about the contents of the packages?''

''She didn't deliver nothing.''

''I think she did, and also began asking questions—awkward questions without acceptable answers. Suddenly it became vital to win her trust by lavishing attention on her. Roses, naughty suggestions to make her feel desirable, little picnics in the office, a fabricated undercover cop—whatever it took to keep her from wondering about her clandestine meetings with Marcus near the campus.''

''That's a bunch of shit. I haven't had anything to do with Marcus for a couple of weeks. You heard me telling him to keep out of the center. He may have hung around the parking lot out front, but it was because he was waiting for Bobbi to bring out a bag of goodies.''

Sighing, I turned to Peter. ''A couple of nights ago Marcus parked at the far end of the lot—not to pick up Bobbi after class, but to pick up a package from Jody since Maribeth was no longer available. I was sitting on the hood of my car when Jody appeared on the sidewalk and said he'd stepped out for a cigarette. If he'd stepped out through the front door, I definitely would have noticed. When he ducked back in to get matches, the music nearly blew me off the car.''

''Mrs. Malloy's taste is somewhat antiquated,'' Peter explained to the group. ''Concertos, sonatas, etudes, but not hard rock.''

Jody took out a cigarette and stuck it between his lips. ''So sometimes I go out the back door and come around the side. What's the big deal?''

''Marcus probably figured the police were getting suspicious, and said as much to you,'' I continued. ''Then Bobbi discovered that a real live policeman had been working out in the weight room, and that the two new members of the teen class seemed to be pals of his. She bounced over to the hospital and quizzed Maribeth about the potassium and some of the other symptoms. As a physical education major, she was familiar with the signs of steroids and was aware of the athletic department scandal. Maribeth was the link. Did Bobbi finally put the pieces together and come back here to confront you? Is that why you shot her and dumped her in the Jacuzzi?''

"She attacked me. You were there."

"Not in the sense Edward R. Murrow meant, no offense intended," I said, shaking my head. "You said you heard something and went off to investigate. You claimed to have been hit on the head, but I didn't see or hear anyone. But you wanted a witness to back up your story, so you insisted on going to the office, where you conveniently discovered the telephone was dead. You emphasized what danger you would be in, then went storming into the dark with a gun. You caught my attention in the weight room and made sure I came to warn you. You darted through the door that led to the men's dressing room, fired the gun, and came back to relate how Bobbi had grabbed your wrist and caused the gun to go off. Maybe you thought the hot water might prevent the coroner from determining the time of death. It might have worked, but there was too much blood in the Jacuzzi, Jody. Too much blood."

Peter said to Jorgeson, "Have all the men search for a bullet hole in the wall of one of the rooms. Also, have the fingerprint guy dust the handles of this bag for prints. I'm sure our friend was careful not to leave any prints on the drug paraphernalia or on the key, but he was in a bit of a hurry this time and he might have been careless."

"You don't have anything on me," Jody said. "So I held Bobbi's bag for her one time, and maybe somebody fired a shot before I even leased the building. Maribeth's the one who killed someone, not Joseph Delano."

"Maribeth did lost control of her car at an unfortunate moment," I said, thinking of one of Peter's many smartass remarks. "By that evening she was having a difficult time because of the steroids. She went into what's been called a roid rage, drove off, and then stopped at the red light. It was six o'clock, time for the news. If we could get a transcript of the radio broadcast, I think we'd hear the story about the scandal at the college athletic department, about the athlete whose heart attack was caused by steroid abuse. Something clicked, and she came back not to confront Candice or me, but to confront you and to demand an explanation. Her heightened agitation provoked the heart attack."

Peter gave me a facetiously wondering look. "Malloy strikes again. I'll interview Maribeth in the morning. Once she learns that Jody was dosing her with steroids, she may have things to tell us about his transactions with the campus liaison. Jorgeson, escort our friend out to the car, read him his rights, and take him to the station so he can contact a lawyer. He most definitely will need one."

Jorgeson, Jody, and the doorman departed. I sat down behind the desk and allowed myself a smile.

"Pleased with yourself?" Peter murmured.

"How long have you suspected the steroids were coming from here?" I countered sweetly. "If you'd bothered to tell me the truth a few days ago, I'd have been discreet. But you insisted Maribeth's crash was an accident, and I felt obliged to prove otherwise."

"While nearly getting yourself killed. Has it occurred to you that Jody might not have been finished setting the stage for the police? He had another bullet in the gun, and we might have found two bodies in the Jacuzzi and heard a story about Bobbi shooting you before her struggle with Jody."

I was in too good a mood to entertain silly hypothetical remarks. "What did Gerald have to say about the ladder?"

"Nothing. The last I heard he was still curled up on the braided rug in the foyer, snoring like a hippo with a sinus infection. I have someone watching the house."

"The little old lady with the German shepherd?"

"Officers Vonna Montgomery and Killer Instinct strolled up to the house after you left." He sat down across from me, crossed his legs, folded his hands in his lap, and produced a smile of such honied benevolence that I wanted to duck under the desk. "We would have gotten to Delano within a week, you know. We're plodders, but we and the feds and the NCAA investigators were all plodding in the right direction—when you stirred things up with your mulish insistence and meddlesome questions. If you'd behaved yourself, the Rodriquez girl wouldn't have become involved to the point that she wanted to be paid for her silence."

"She was upset when she came out of the office at seven-thirty," I said frowning.

"Jody was gone at the time. Marcus was in there, and must have told her what he'd done to your car."

"Someone peeked through the window of the Book Depot that morning. I presumed it was a customer, but he might have wanted to ascertain I was occupied elsewhere. If Bobbi wasn't involved with the drug racket, then why would he tell her what he did?"

"She was getting suspicious, and he wanted to scare her. We picked him up earlier in the evening."

"Why?"

"I had someone plod over to your garage. The cotter pin was lying on the floor, doing its best to look as if it fell out of its own accord. We found a partial print, and ran it. It seems Marcus has a record, mostly juvenile, but with a few more mature incidents. We plodded over to the athletic dorm and invited him to visit with us for a spell. He wanted to sing all night, but I had to disappoint him by coming here to find out what the feisty, foolhardy heroine was doing in a dark building with a suspected drug dealer."

"Whatever sent you on such a wild-goose chase?"

"Joanie Powell called me and told me you were acting very strange. She was sure you were lying about something."

I sighed. "There goes my exquisite hand-built vase for the mantel."

"Perhaps she'll give it to me so that I can put it on my mantel," Peter said. "The mantel above the fireplace, that is. The fireplace that could provide a flickering fire to be admired from the sofa over the rim of a wineglass. I would like to think you might live long enough to share the scenario, but you do seem determined to plunge yourself into trouble, don't you?''

"Oh, dear, are you angry with me? I was just trying to help, Lieutenant.''

"And I was just trying to—'' He stopped and rubbed his eyes, then said, "Never mind. It's after midnight. Leave Joanie's car here and I'll drive you home. That way I can be sure you won't stop at a convenience store in the middle of a holdup, or pick up a hitchhiker who turns out to be an escaped felon with a machine gun and a yen to see Mexico.''

"I warned Caron that I might not be home until dawn.''

"Did you?''

"I did.''

"That was clever.''

I smiled modestly. "I thought so, but I'm keenly aware of my brilliant deductive prowess.''

"Perhaps if I saw more of you, I would be, too.''

"An interesting hypothesis, and worthy of further exploration. Shall we go?''

About the Author

Joan Hess lives and writes in Fayetteville, Arkansas. Her previous books in the Claire Malloy series are *Strangled Prose*, *The Murder at the Murder at the Mimosa Inn*, *Dear Miss Demeanor,* and *A Really Cute Corpse*.
A Diet to Die For won the American Mystery Award for the Best Traditional Mystery of 1989.

THE LATEST
JOAN HESS
MYSTERIES
FEATURING
THE ENIGMATIC
CLAIRE MALLOY